FINDING THE SNOWDON LILY

Catrin Owen's father, a guide on Snowdon, shows botanists the sites of rare plants. He wants his daughter to marry Taran Davies. But then the attractive photographer Philip Meredith and his sister arrive, competing to be first to photograph the 'Snowdon Lily' in its secret location. His arrival soon has Catrin embroiled in the race, and she finds her life, as well as her heart, at stake. For the coveted prize generates treachery amongst the rivals — and Taran's jealousy . . .

Books by Heather Pardoe
in the Linford Romance Library:

HER SECRET GARDEN
THE IVORY PRINCESS
THE SOARING HEART
THE EAGLE STONE
THE THEATRE ON THE PIER

HEATHER PARDOE

FINDING THE SNOWDON LILY

Complete and Unabridged

LINFORD
Leicester

First published in Great Britain in 2006

First Linford Edition
published 2008

British Library CIP Data

Pardoe, Heather
Finding the Snowdon Lily.—Large print ed.—
Linford romance library
1. Rare plants—Fiction 2. Snowdon (Wales)
—Fiction 3. Love stories 4. Large type books
I. Title
823.9′2 [F]

ISBN 978–1–84782–108–9

Published by
F. A. Thorpe (Publishing)
Anstey, Leicestershire

Set by Words & Graphics Ltd.
Anstey, Leicestershire
Printed and bound in Great Britain by
T. J. International Ltd., Padstow, Cornwall

This book is printed on acid-free paper

1

'The Grey King is down on the mountain again, then.' Catrin Owen paused on the rough pathway of stones, and turned in the direction of the voice echoing towards her through the mist. All around her nothing could be seen, just the thick wall of white that seemed to have shut away everything beyond the long grasses laden with heavy droplets that had already dampened the rim of her dress, and soaked their way through her boots. Catrin pushed back her bonnet, and brushed cold moisture from her face.

It had been a perfect June dawn that day, bright and clear as glass. The ridges of Snowdon towering above the little valley had been etched against the clean blue, seemingly sharp enough to cut the eye. Then, just before noon, the bank of white had appeared from nowhere, as it so often did, creeping round the peaks, and spilling over into slow damp swirls that transformed the world into shadow.

'So he is,' returned Catrin, as the cloud in front of her thinned a little to reveal the dark silhouettes of Rhys Evans, and his son, Guto, repairing one of the dry stone walls that stretched right the way up the hillside.

'Chasing the visitors, no doubt,' called Guto, with a chuckle. 'He'll have them off that mountain soon enough.'

Catrin glanced up to the shape of Crib Goch ridge, the narrowest and most terrifying route up to Snowdon's summit, looming slowly into view. In the eerie silence voices could be heard high above, accompanied by the abrupt rattled of dislodged stones. She shivered.

Ever since she was small she had heard the stories of the Brenin Llwyd, the Grey King, who came down in the mist to torment and pursue strangers on the mountains to their deaths. Today she wished she had never heard the tales at all. Rhys gave his son a reproving nudge with his elbow.

'Your dad up there then, is he, Catrin?' he asked, gently.

'Yes,' she replied. 'He took a party from Chester up this morning. They started at dawn, they should be up on the summit by now.'

'Ah, he'll be fine, just you see, Catrin *bach*. The old Brenin Llwyd won't touch a Snowdon man born and bred, and your dad's the best guide in the business.'

And so he was. There were times when Catrin secretly wished that he wasn't. Any tourist who took the trouble to ask would always be directed to Will Owen as the guide who knew the best routes up the mountain, and who could answer any question you cared to ask on the history, or the flora and fauna of the area. Good guides were hard to come by.

In the past few years the railways had reached the mountainous wilderness of

North Wales, bringing with them flocks of tourists from England, and even farther afield, eager to sample the romantic wilderness described by Wordsworth and painted by Turner.

Prime Minister Gladstone swore by his retreats to Penmaenmawr, just along the coast, and new books were printed every year describing in what Dad laughingly called 'the purplest of purple' prose the awe-inspiring experience of climbing the higher peaks.

There were plenty of bad guides to be had, ones who just knew the more obvious paths to the summit, but, with the little idea of the names of the surrounding mountains were quite likely to make it up as they went along, with the odd piece of the Austrian Alps thrown in for good measure.

Dad always cursed them, as giving all guides a bad name, and he would take up any party, whatever the weather, rather than leave them to the not-so-tender mercies of such rogues, who were not above taking their client's money, and then abandoning them when the weather closed in.

Dad would never abandon anyone. Catrin tore her eyes away from the ridge, where the mist was once again thickening until it was almost invisible, and forced herself to sound as cheerful as possible.

'I know. He'll have them back for their evening meal, and a good strong pint of *cwrw* to help them recover. They'll probably be asking to go up Tryfan or the Glyders before the evening is out.' Rhys chuckled, while Guto grinned, and took a few steps down towards the path. He was a large, clumsily-built young man, with a mass of unruly fair curls framing his weathered face.

'You going up to the guest house then, Catrin?' he asked, shyly, even though this was a journey he saw her make very day.

'Yes,' she replied, finding his awkwardness catching. She liked Guto, whose great rough hands that could lift the sharpest of boulders without a scratch could also be surprisingly gentle when it came to a lamb in trouble, or a child with a grazed knee.

Only, this past year, since she had turned seventeen and quite old enough to be considered as a possible wife, she had found him eyeing her with a new interest. He hadn't yet found the courage to ask her to stand up with him at the village dance, or even to walk to the lake and back, but he was working his way up to it; this might be all new to her, but even Catrin could see that.

Guto might not be rich, and could well be forced to start his married life in his parent's tumble-down shack high up amongst the sheep-fields above Llanberis, but there were worse men in the village a girl could choose. Or be forced into choosing . . . She smiled.

'Uncle doesn't have any guests at the moment, but there are sure to be plenty of climbers up on Snowdon today ready for a hot meal when they come down.'

'Oh.' He cleared his throat. 'I'm sure

your cooking is the best they've ever tasted,' he added, which, for him, was bold.

'Well thank you for the compliment, Guto.' She couldn't quite control the faintly mischievous twitch to her lips at the thought of the ridiculous sight of them standing in the mist on a bare hillside while Guto desperately tried to find the words to be a knight in shining armour, straight from a storybook. 'I'm sure they're more used to expensive restaurants and find my dishes very plain.' She saw him take a deep breath.

'Well I'm sure I wouldn't,' he replied, his voice deepening. He took a step closer. 'Catrin — '

'*Duw*, boy, you going to be chatting there all day?' It was his father, growing cold and impatient at this pause in repairing the wall, and quite blind to the courageous move his son was just about to make. 'It's a proper old woman you're turning out to be. You'll be getting Catrin late to her work, you've all evening to be talking to her.'

'I'll speak to you soon, Guto,' said Catrin, gently, trying to ease his obvious humiliation. She busily adjusted the basket on her arm. 'I'm afraid I must go, or I really will be late.'

He nodded and stepped back. As he did so the mist came back down around him, so that even before he had turned to rejoin his father he had vanished from her sight.

Despite it being almost Midsummer's Day, it was cold in the mist. She might be well below the summit, but Catrin was high above sea level, where the warmth began to leave the air. She made this journey every day in the summer, from the little stone cottage tucked into the hillsides just above the stretch of lake that covered much of the lower part of the valley, reflecting the ruined castle of Dolbadarn and the lower reaches of Snowdon in its still, dark waters.

The small guesthouse at the top of Pen-y-pass, where many walkers began their attempt on the summit, had been run by her Uncle John for several years now, providing hot meals for the returning adventurers, and a few rooms for guests brave enough to stay in the very heart of the mountains, or for unfortunates caught out by the weather and unable to return to their hotels in the more civilised surroundings of the valleys.

When the old cook had finally found it too much to make the trek up the mountain every day from the village of Llanberis, which lay far below on the shores of the lake, Catrin had been glad to step in. Money was never plentiful in the Owen household, and the work made a welcome supplement to Dad's earnings as a guide.

As she reached the top of the pass, the mist swept aside once, stirred by a rising breeze. For a moment the stone walls and slate roof of the little guesthouse sparkled in an unexpected ray of sunshine. Catrin paused, her attention caught by the dramatic fall of mountainside in front of her, down into the next valley, and the village of Beddgelert far below.

On the narrow winding road that made its way through the mountains a coach and horses were struggling slowly upwards towards the pass.

There was a clear view of the summit of Snowdon from one of the larger bends, not that these visitors were ever likely to benefit from it.

Pushing the thought of the coach, and the unfortunate tourists who had suffered the uncomfortable journey, rattled and bumped by bends and potholes, for nothing, from her mind, Catrin brushed the moisture from her coat and bonnet once more, and made her way inside.

* * *

'That'll be them. I was beginning to think they'd changed their minds, or the train had never arrived.' John Owen grinned cheerfully at his niece, and stirred the fire into life.

'The coach is coming here?' There had been no mention of new guests when she had left here last night.

'That's right. Two guests. A telegram arrived late last night.' He rubbed his hands. 'The wonders of modern technology, eh? Just a few hours and a message arrived here from London. It used to take the Irish Mail coach an entire day when I was a boy, and that seemed miracle enough in those days.'

'How long are they staying, Uncle?' At least the beds had been changed, and the rooms aired. Catrin began to make a mental note of what they would need. They would be nearly here by now, there was not much time.

'A week. Maybe more. They're on some kind of mission, it seems.'

'Mission?' What kind of mission could it be that would take them halfway up Snowdon in the mist?

'Mr Meredith didn't say. Though I don't expect it is a usual kind of one. The family is known to be quite eccentric, you know.

'Oh.' Catrin stopped her note-taking, and raised her eyebrows.

'I knew them that time I was working in London. Not well, of course, but Philip Meredith always seemed a very steady young man. He'd just taken up this new thing of photography, you should have seen the people flocking to have a look in that studio of his. Fascinating. Now that's modern technology for you; pictures made out of light.'

'Is he coming to make photographs here, do you think?' Catrin was intrigued. They'd had a photographer come through the village a few years ago, with his cumbersome equipment for taking and processing pictures all contained inside a covered wagon.

She'd had a quick look inside, it was almost completely dark, with rows of bottles looming out of the gloom, and an acrid smell of chemicals. She had a sudden vision of the coach she had seen filled to the brim with photographic equipment that would spill out the moment the door was opened, and hastily suppressed a giggle.

'I've never met the sister at all,' her uncle was continuing. 'Though I heard all about her, of course. She was all over the newspapers at the time.' He grinned. 'I believe it drove old Mr Meredith to distraction. I rather think he considers women should be at home with a family rather than spending their time in the Swiss Alps climbing every peak they could find. Not to mention with half the English press at her heels.'

Catrin blinked. Dad often had one or two women in the parties of visitors he guided up the mountains, but she'd never met a woman who took the sport so seriously. The Swiss Alps were much higher than even Snowdon. And this adventurous woman was coming to stay here. Dad would just love to hear this. She stopped in her tracks, remembering again where Dad was at this very moment. The fire next to her sent a small burst of smoke into the room, accompanied by the whistling of wind in the chimneys, and the creak of rafters.

'Sounds like a proper storm brewing,' she murmured, as she made her way to the kitchen at the back of the house. If a storm came now, with Dad and his party right at the very summit. She swallowed, finding a bitter taste in her mouth, to go with the knot hardening in her belly. Dad had survived such storms before, she told herself. And worse. He'd been out once on Christmas Day in a blizzard, when the snow had drifted waist high in places, to rescue a climber lost on the mountain. He'd survived that, and brought the man down to safety.

He'd be back, she told herself, firmly. In a few hours he'd be sitting by the fire, a mug of hot tea in his hands, watching Mr Meredith's adventurous daughter with those clear blue eyes of his. He'd be back. She was sure of it.

2

'The Snowdon Lily?' John Owen eyed his newly-arrived guests in surprise, and scratched his head.

'Yes. *Lloydia serotina.* The Snowdon Lily. Have you ever seen it?'

'I'm afraid not, miss.' Judith Meredith gave an impatient sigh at these words, and looked around the main sitting room of the little guest-house as if she suddenly found it small and shabby.

Catrin eyed her from the corner of her eye as she placed the tray with the best tea-things down on the table. Judith Meredith was a tall young woman, broad shouldered, but slender, with blue-grey eyes, and a mass of fair hair corralled firmly into a bun behind her head. Even Catrin's inexpert eye could tell that the cut and the material of the dark green travelling dress were the best money could buy.

The gloves the young lady was stripping carelessly from her hands, as if she could bear the feel of them no more, were of the softest kid, with stitching so fine as to be scarcely visible, while Judith's manner spoke of one used to having her every whim obeyed.

Her eyes met those of the young man rubbing his hands together in the warmth of the fire, as if attempting to get some feeling back into them. Philip Meredith was darker than his sister, his eyes more blue than grey, and they were, she discovered, watching her closely, almost as if he were attempting to read her every thought.

As the only woman who could be called *young* working at the guest house, Catrin was used to deflecting the attentions of young men, particularly those celebrating a successful ascent with rather too much of the local beer, and she was making no exceptions even for a rather intriguing photographer who had appeared with only a large knapsack rather than an entire coach-load of equipment, something she was just dying to question him about.

She returned his gaze as severely as she knew how, and concentrated on pouring the tea.

'But you must have met some who have seen it.' Judith was clearly not giving up her questioning easily.

'One or two, miss. It's very rare, and it grows only in places dangerous to visit. Places not many climbers will risk. Several have been killed in the attempt, you see.'

'Yes, yes, I know,' she replied, brushing this aside. 'But you can tell us where these men are to be found?'

'Judith!' put in Philip, quietly. 'We've only just arrived. I'm sure Mr Owen has got better things to do than be badgered to death on the subject of botany.'

'It's what we came for,' she retorted. 'And we haven't much time. It's no use putting this off.'

'Well, I think I'd quite like to settle for tea first,' he returned with a smile. 'You'll have to excuse my sister,' he added, lightly, 'the word, 'stubborn' was invented for her.'

'Don't be ridiculous,' snapped Judith, irritably. 'All I'm enquiring after is a guide, and he must be used to that.' She turned back to John. 'Didn't you say your brother is a guide?'

'Yes, miss. One of the best.'

'Well, then.'

'But I wouldn't know if he's found the site of the Snowdon Lily. I'm not much of a mountaineer myself, I'm afraid.'

He gestured towards Catrin, who having finished pouring the tea was making her escape from those watchful blue eyes as quickly as she knew how. 'You'd be better asking that of my niece.'

'Really?' Now there were two pairs of eyes watching her closely. Judith, Catrin had already decided, was the kind of young woman who never noticed anyone who was not of use to her in some way or other.

Having discovered Catrin was the unexpected source of the information she was looking for, she was now eyeing her as closely as her brother.

Catrin cleared her throat uncomfortably, these two could drag a girl into all sorts of trouble in their different ways, she told herself, seeing the determined look on Judith Meredith's face.

'He has found the Snowdon Lily,' she offered, hoping they would then leave her alone. 'Several times. Once at the base of Clogwyn Du'r Arddau, on Snowdon, and the other on the Clyders, on the other side of the valley.'

'And he was sure it was the lily?' demanded Judith.

'Yes.'

'Absolutely certain?'

'Judith! I'm sure Miss Owen knows what she's talking about.'

'Well, we need to be certain. We can't afford to make any mistakes about this.'

'Quite sure,' said Catrin, firmly. 'The

time on Snowdon he was working as a guide for a professor of Botany from Cardiff University. I've made some drawings, you can see them if you want to make absolutely certain.'

'Drawings?' This time it was Philip questioning her, and it would have been hard to miss the touch of disapproval in his voice. 'From a specimen?'

'No, of course not,' she retorted, stung. 'Do you think we don't know any better than that? My father never allows anyone to pick the lily. With so many collectors there would soon be none left.'

'You mean you were there?'

'Yes,' she returned, lifting her chin defiantly. Let him show one inch of being disbelieving, or scandalised, and she'd not speak a word to him ever again — beyond what was strictly necessary, of course. Which, she suddenly decided, was probably the best thing, given that smile of his which was just a little too charming for comfort . . . But Catrin was not about to be saved, instead she found he was laughing.

'Well, Judith,' he was saying, 'it looks as if you've met your match at last. Another female mountaineer, and one who doesn't see fit to make a fuss about it.'

'I'm not really a mountaineer, I've only climbed here, not in the Alps, or anything nearly so ambitious,' said Catrin, feeling rather foolish, and even more uneasy at the way Philip Meredith was continuing to watch her so closely, without even trying to hide the fact.

'But you can still help us,' said Judith, who really did seem to have a one-track mind.

'Me?'

'Oh yes, we're going to need all the help we can get. Philip's knapsack weighs quite enough on its own, we are going to be very slow getting all our equipment up there.'

'Equipment?' Catrin eyed the knapsack, which had not been left with the other luggage, but carefully placed within view in a corner of the room. It was large, but not nearly the size of a wagon.

'Yes. His photographic equipment. To take the picture of the lily.'

'You are intending to photograph the Snowdon Lily?' demanded Catrin's uncle, who seemed to have just decided that his guests were both quite mad.

'Of course,' replied Judith. 'And we have to work as fast as we can before anyone else gets there first.'

'There are others?' John Owen had clearly concluded the whole world had gone mad.

'Yes, of course,' said Judith, impatiently. 'With that kind of prize there must be hundreds heading this way.'

'I'm sure not hundreds,' remarked Philip, who seemed to be finding all this faintly amusing.

'Well, enough. And we've got to get there first. We've just got to.'

'What my sister means, is that she has to,' explained Philip, dryly. 'And since I've had the misfortune to make photography my profession, I shall be dragged along behind her.'

He smiled at John Owen, who was still watching him suspiciously. 'Blame the Royal Cambrian Botanical society. They've offered a substantial reward for the first photograph of the Snowdon Lily. Substantial enough, that is, to fund Judith's next expedition to the Alps.

'I'm afraid our father has given up seeing mountaineering as something she needs to get out of her system, and has just produced a prospective husband rather than the necessary funds.'

'Husband!' snorted Judith. 'A Banker! A Banker. Who only ever talks about facts and figures, and doesn't consider I have any brain at all. Father knows Richard Sullivan is the last man I'd ever consider marrying. He's just trying to make a point, and make me do as he wishes. But if I can just do this climb, I'll have the newspapers cover everything about it. That will bring me backers, if nothing else will.'

She turned to Catrin, her eyes

suddenly pleading, with a desperation Catrin had never thought to see in their depths. 'So we've got to do this, you see. We've got to find the Snowdon Lily and be the first to get a photograph back to London. Or I'll be forced to suffocate as Mrs Sullivan for the rest of my life.'

'I'm sure my father will guide you,' said Catrin. Miss Meredith didn't seem quite so fierce all of a sudden, and Catrin could understand the pressures that could be put on a young woman to marry a man would never have chosen for herself.

Dad was a kind and generous father, but these last few years he had started to make non-too-subtle plans for his daughter. Catrin knew he meant it for the best. As he said himself, he was not growing any younger, and the life of a guide in the harsh environment of the mountains was not an easy one.

If only he had not got it into his head that Taran Davies was a reliable young man, and exactly the kind to suit her.

Taran and his father ran the Snowdon Hotel in Llanberis, and had prospered lately from the influx of visitors brought in by the new roads and the railways. So much so that Taran would be giving up working as a guide after this season.

'Don't marry a guide, *cariad*,' Dad had told her so many times she had lost count. 'It's a hard life, for a wife, never knowing if her man is coming home or not. It wore your mam out before her time. She never complained, but I knew it did. I'm sure that's what killed her in the end. Whatever you do, never marry a guide.'

Or a farmer, he would certainly add if he had seen Guto's shy intentions this morning. A farmer's wife was worn out by relentless hard work in all weathers, he would say, just as surely as the wife of a guide was worn out by anxiety. No, Dad would never consider Guto as a possible suitor.

Catrin shivered, despite the warmth of the fire. What was it about Taran? He was young, good looking, and wealthier than most men in the surrounding area. Girls from miles around were envious of the obvious attention he had been giving her these past few months. She could not have done better, even if she had schemed to land the biggest catch in the valley as a husband.

And love, they said, came, even if it was not there to begin with, and she was no empty-headed miss who dreamed only of Prince Charming. And yet . . . She looked up and found the clear blue eyes of Philip Meredith scrutinising her face, almost as if he really could see into her heart and read her doubts.

'Taran!' She jumped at her uncle's exclamation. Surely he couldn't read her thoughts, too? But her uncle's eyes were fixed on the open door to the sitting room, where the figure of a man stood, dripping water slowly on to the floor. 'Taran! Good heavens, man. Where are the others?'

'Just behind me,' replied the new-comer, stepping further into the room, although not before Catrin had caught a glimpse of his dark eyes fixed intently on Philip Meredith's face.

'Thank heavens!' exclaimed John. 'We thought you'd not be down for hours, yet.' But Catrin did not join his relief.

The grim expression on Taran's face had not lessened, even though he appeared to be putting Mr Meredith from his mind. And there was no sign of her father rushing in behind him to reassure her. Catrin's stomach tightened into one huge knot.

'Taran? What is it? Is it Dad?'

'Your dad's fine, Catrin. He stayed up there. One of the visitors slipped on the rocks when the mist came down. Looks like a broken leg, a bad one. We tried to carry him, but — ' He gave a contemptuous nod of his head towards the exhausted and bedraggled figures making their way into the room behind him — 'they didn't prove much use. I brought them down before they did any more damage to themselves. It's getting bad out there, we'll need some real mountaineers to get the injured one down.'

As if to prove his point, a howl of wind went through the rafters, setting them creaking as if they were in half a mind to lift themselves off, and send the slates scattering.

'I'll need to borrow your horse, John.'

'Of course. Take what you need. There'll be plenty of men in the farms who'll gladly go back up with you.'

'And we need to get word to the guides at Capel Curig. They're the most experienced.'

'But that will take hours!' exclaimed Catrin.

'No good going up, now. Thank heaven we're nearly at the longest day. By the time I get the men assembled it will be starting to get light again.'

'I'll go with you,' said Catrin. She found Taran frowning at her.

'Nonsense,' he replied, sharply. 'The mountains are no place for a woman. There are sick men here to look after here. Don't worry, Catrin, I'll bring your father back for you.'

He put a hand on her arm: for a moment she thought he was trying to reassure her, but then she caught the quick glance in Philip's direction. A time like this, and Taran was laying down ownership of her for the benefit a man who had looked once in her direction!

Anger flooded through her distress as she watched Taran make his way towards the door, and in a flash her mind became utterly clear. That was what she had always mistrusted about him, the way he treated her as if she were merely a silly child, charming, but quite unable to deal with the ways of the world. That, and the way he clearly assumed she would never refuse him when it suited him to ask.

'And they say ignorance is bliss,' remarked Judith next to her, rather more loudly than was necessary. Catrin saw his back stiffen, and he paused at the door as, unable by any social rule imaginable to challenge a woman himself, he waited for Catrin to rush to his defence. She remained silent. Taran waited a moment longer, and then vanished into the night.

In that moment Catrin knew she could never marry him — though if Dad were injured in the night, or worse, she might be faced with little other choice.

She found a hand placed firmly on her arm, and turned to find Judith smiling at her, with a positively wicked glint to her eye. Yes indeed, thought Catrin, Judith Meredith could get a girl into a whole lot of trouble without even trying.

'I'd better get the blankets,' she muttered. The less time she had to think about anything for the next few hours, the better.

'And I'll make the tea, hot and plenty of it,' said Judith. She raised her eyebrows as Catrin started to protest. 'You think I've never been in a kitchen before? What do you think I do when

I'm camping out in the hills? There you have to build your own fireplace before you even begin.'

'What did I tell you? Stubborn,' said Philip.

Despite everything, Catrin laughed. She had a feeling that, for better or worse, her life would change forever this night. The crash of rain flung harshly against the windowpanes brought her back again.

'Heaven help anyone caught out in that tonight,' said Judith quietly, serious once more.

Heaven help them indeed, thought Catrin.

3

It was the longest night Catrin had ever known. Sleep was impossible, instead, she helped Judith with cups of hot tea, until the two guests, worn out with their long journey, bumped and rattled in the coach across the potholes of the road, made their way to bed.

With the little guesthouse quiet and still, Catrin found the wind whining amongst the rafters and rattling at the slates impossible to ignore. Uncle John dozed in his armchair, fully dressed and ready for action at any moment.

She retreated to the little kitchen at the far end of the house to bake endless loaves of bread in the oven set deep in the wall next to the iron range, along with solid slabs of Bara Brith, crammed as full as she could make them with dried fruit, for Taran and his team of rescuers to take with them in the morning.

The wind and rain battered the little hut all through the night, making those who had been fortunate to make their way down to its shelter turn restlessly in their sleep, as they huddled exhausted in front of Uncle John's blazing fire.

As the first light crept through the racing clouds, Taran returned with three of his fellow guides from Capel Curig, just a few miles along the valley. They stomped in, wet and windblown from the ride across the open moorland, weathered cheeks reddened by the cold.

'More like winter, it is,' muttered Jac Morgan, the oldest and most experienced of the guides, holding his large, muscular hands out to the flames. He caught Catrin's gaze, and smiled, '*Duw*, Catrin, but I've been up there in worse, and so has your dad. It's the times you have the snow and the ice to fight against, that's the time you worry.'

Catrin smiled back. 'I know. Dad'll be fine, I know he will.'

‘No sign of it clearing.’ Taran came in, brushing the wet from his hair. ‘We’d best be going, then.’

‘Aye, that we should. The sooner we get them down the better.’ Jac pressed his hands so close to the flames a slight smell of singeing pervaded the room, before, with just the slightest of regretful sighs, striding over to his backpack, waiting ready for him next to the door. ‘Thank you, *cariad*.’ He took the hunk of warm bread and cheese, wrapped tight in a cloth along with thick slices of the Bara Brith from Catrin with a smile.

‘And this.’ Catrin held out a second package. ‘For Dad. And for the man up with him, if he’s able to eat.’

‘I’ll make sure they get it,’ smiled Jac. ‘They’ll be hungry after a night on the mountain. Nothing like good home-cooked food to give them energy.’

Catrin smiled at the kindness in his tone. Dad and Jac had worked together for many years. If anyone could find Dad and get him down to safety in this weather, it was Jac Morgan. She handed packages to the rest of the mountaineers, handing over the last one to Taran, waiting impatiently by the door.

'Don't you worry, we'll find him, Catrin.' From the moment he arrived, Taran had been bustling about, full of his own importance as leader of this expedition, quite ignoring the fact that it was older, and far more experienced men he would be leading.

'I know you will.' Catrin withdrew her hand quickly from the grasp that threatened to claim her. Whatever happened in the next few hours, she suddenly saw, Taran was ensuring he would be seen as the leader of this rescue attempt. Whether Dad came down alive, or dead, or even possibly horribly injured, everyone would always know she was in Taran's debt.

From the corner of her eye she caught Jac Morgan frowning. Jac understood that, too. She swallowed. 'I'll be ready for you when you return,' she said. 'There will be hot soup all ready, for all of you.' Then she turned and walked smartly towards the kitchen, taking care not to take one glance back towards the men making their way out of the door and into the storm.

'Doesn't it ever stop raining here?' Judith Meredith paused in her pacing of the room, and gazed through the small glass panes at the cloud swirling around the little guesthouse, obliterating everything but a few miserable-looking sheep bracing themselves against the wind.

'We're high up amongst the mountains, what else do you expect?' replied her brother, looking up from polishing the selection of lenses set out carefully before him with a good-humoured smile.

'But it might last for weeks.'

'Unlikely, I should think. Why, in that case, would visitors be flocking here? Isn't that true, Miss Owen?'

Catrin paused in her mission of taking bed linen up to the guestrooms.

There were no more guests booked in for the next two days, but the restless energy that had been with her all through the hours of darkness would not let her go.

'The weather here is very changeable,' she said, quietly.

'There, you see. The word of an expert.'

'I'm hardly an expert.'

'It sounds to me as if you know these mountains better than most. That, in my book, makes you an expert,' he retorted.

Despite the heaviness on her heart, Catrin found herself smiling. Philip Meredith was no doubt known as a charmer, in his own circles. With those dark eyes of his, and his slow, wide, smile, he most probably had every woman he could care to name worshipping at his feet.

Catrin had seen many visitors pass through Uncle John's guesthouse, with many a would-be charmer amongst them. She wasn't about to fall for dark eyes and a pleasant smile, but today she was in no mood to brush aside a friendly face. Today, she considered, she needed all the friends she could get.

'In that case, I'll take your word for it,' she returned. She paused, her eyes straying to the wooden box, beautifully constructed, lying on the table, a selection of round glass lenses, surrounded by metal, laid out carefully around it.

'Are you interested in photography, Miss Owen?'

She blushed as she caught his inquiring glance. 'No. Not really. At least, I don't know much about it. I expect it is far more usual in the city.'

'Oh, far more. I'm having to fight for customers to come and have their portrait taken in my studio, with so many growing up around me.' He grinned. 'I can see this could be a new career my sister has opened up to me. Landscapes, particularly of wild and exotic places, are in great demand.'

Catrin blinked. 'Is Snowdon exotic?'

'Of course. Mr Wordsworth's poems and Mr Turner's paintings have much to answer for. The great wilderness, where you can be at one with nature. These mountains are as wild as any I've seen.'

Catrin eyed him. He seemed perfectly serious, but she was not entirely sure if he was teasing her, or not.

'I thought people would prefer Switzerland, or places like that. Aren't the mountains much bigger there?'

'Taller, yes. But wilder? I don't know. And from what we saw yesterday from the coach, these are certainly as beautiful.'

'Oh,' said Catrin. 'So you are going to take photographs of the mountains.'

'Naturally.' His eyes followed hers as she surveyed the equipment spread out before him. 'Although it will be hard work, I agree. And I'm not entirely certain just how successful this portable equipment will be.'

'I thought you told me you'd been using it for the past month?' snapped

Judith, her attention distracted from the window.

'In the civilised surroundings of Hyde Park and Bayswater, yes. But on the top of a windswept mountain — well, I've never tried that before.'

'But it's got to work. It's got to! You should have told me, Philip. I would have hired someone who did have the skill.'

'I hate to remind you, Judith,' he retorted, acidly, 'but you couldn't afford to pay them. And who else would spend their summer holidays hauling half their bodyweight around on their backs for fresh air and love?'

Judith flushed bright red. Philip winced, as if ashamed of his sudden burst of irritability. 'Not that there is anything wrong with fresh air,' he added in gentler tones.

'You didn't have to come if you didn't want to.'

'I came because I did want to. I told you, I'm sick and tired of dressing up rich society ladies with nothing better to do as Greek goddesses and setting them amongst pillars with their yappy little Pekes still on their knees. I shall lose fingers to one of those little devils, one day. That or the spoilt children they insist against all reasonable evidence to the contrary are perfectly well behaved.'

He caught Catrin's wide eyes and gave a wry smile. 'Aha, and you thought the life of a high street photographer was a glamorous one, Miss Owen? You try and keep some spoilt brat gazing soulfully between angel's wings for a full three minutes for the plate to expose. Now that, I can assure you, would try the patience of a saint.'

Catrin grinned. 'Are there many who want their children photographed as angels, then?'

'Mainly the ones who have raised the worst behaved,' he returned, ruefully. He took up another lens and began inspecting it. 'I shall look forward to lilies, however much they try to hide themselves. At least I can be fairly sure they will not bite.'

Catrin moved a little closer, overcome with curiosity. 'Is that what makes the photograph?'

'Part of it. The lens fits on the front of this box, like so. That concentrates the image on to the photographic plate at the back.'

'And it really is just light that makes the picture?'

'More or less. This glass plate here is coated with a chemical. You prepare as many as you need beforehand, then slot them in, and when you are ready to take the photograph you uncover the side covered with the light-sensitive chemicals. And there you go.'

'And that's it?' She could scarcely keep the wonder from her voice. So it really was painting with light. Photography was truly a miracle. Philip, however, was grinning.

'Hardly,' he said. 'Once it's exposed, the image on the plate needs to be fixed, or it will vanish before you can get it back to your darkroom. Now that's what's so wonderful about this new equipment.' He nodded to the structure at the far end of the table. 'With this, you can take your darkroom with you on your back.'

Catrin stared at the large box, surrounded by dark material that had been lifted to show rows of little bottles neatly stacked on shelves inside. 'You mean, you are going to carry that up Snowdon?'

'If I want to get a picture of the Snowdon Lily that keeps long enough to make a print for the Cambrian Botanical Society, yes. There is no other way.' He laughed at the expression on her face. 'Miss Owen, if you think I am completely mad, you are quite right. Heaven knows quite how I am going to accomplish this, but I'm certainly going to give it my best try.'

'And there really are others carrying that around on their backs, too, trying to find the lily?'

'I'm afraid so, Miss Owen. This is entirely new equipment, you see. There has never been anything quite so portable before. And since it is impossible to get an entire wagon up to the remote places of mountains, this is the first time the possibility has arisen for the Snowdon Lily to be photographed.'

'Hence the competition,' put in Judith, turning back to the window once more. 'Which we have to win. We just have to.' She paused for a moment, wiping away the frosting of her breath from the damp pane. 'I think the cloud is clearing a little,' she said.

'It is?' The anxiety was back in Catrin, instantly. How could she have forgotten, even for a moment?

'I think so. The rain has lessened, and I can see more of the hillside.'

Forgetting the strangeness of the photographers' trade, Catrin made her way to the door of the house, pulling her coat on as she went. Judith was right. The clouds were retreating fast, leaving streaks of white in the Llanberis Valley below, but revealing the gleam of sun on sea in the far distance, while the mist rolled upwards, uncovering more of the mountainside and the rocky line of the path to the summit at every moment.

'That will make their journey easier for them, *cariad*.' Uncle John was behind her, one hand comfortingly on her shoulder, peering up through the mist with a practiced gaze. 'They'll be down before long, you'll see.'

'I just wish Dad would never have to go back up the mountains at all,' thought Catrin to herself. Out of the corner of her eye she caught sight of Judith, striding past them to look down at the retreating cloud below.

'The wind has changed,' said Uncle John. 'Look, it's coming in from the sea.'

'Yes,' murmured Catrin. Judith heard them, and turned.

'Is that good?'

Uncle John beamed. 'Yes, Miss Meredith. Better chance of fine weather with the wind coming in off the sea. Yes, I'd say it'll be a fine day tomorrow.'

‘Good.’ All thoughts of the rescue taking place in the cliffs above her had clearly been banished from Judith’s mind. ‘So then tomorrow we can begin the search for the Snowdon Lily,’ she said.

4

'I don't know what we would have done without him,' said Dad, stretching his stockinged toes nearer to the fire. 'He's a good man, is Taran. A fine young man.'

'Yes, Dad.' Catrin handed him yet another mug of steaming tea. 'The cawl will be ready in a moment.'

'Ah, now that's what kept me going up there, however wet and cold we were, the thought of your uncle's good fire and your hot soup. I swear I could taste that soup at times. Not that the bread and cheese weren't welcome. I could have sworn I had a deep hole where my belly was by the time Taran reached us.'

'Well, I'm glad you're safe now and Dr Evans says Mr Rowlands will be up and about in a few weeks.'

'So all's well that end's well, eh?'

'Yes, Dad.'

'Well, I shall be glad to be up on that mountain again tomorrow. Can't abide being stuck down here with the weather so fine.'

'You're supposed to be resting!' Catrin eyed her father with a frown. 'It's too soon to be going up again.'

'I can't be letting Taran take my place, cariad. I am the guide here. Young Taran is needed down at his father's hotel in Llanberis. It was good of him to take Miss Meredith and her brother in my place today, but I can't keep him up here. No, no, by tomorrow I shall be fully rested and ready to go. And Taran can drive you down in the cart tonight on his way back.'

'I'd rather stay here.'

'You're needed back down at home. You can't be expecting your nain to be looking after the house forever. Besides, she'll be worrying if you're not down by sunset.'

Catrin sighed. Nain, her grandmother, had stepped in when Mam had died, three years ago. But she was growing old, and finding the keeping of the garden and the hens in the summer while Catrin spent half the week up at the guesthouse and Dad was hardly seen at all, growing harder each year.

Much as she loved working up with the climbers and seeing visitors pass through the guesthouse all summer long, maybe it was time she found a post nearer to home, thought Catrin to herself. Taran had been hinting at an undercook being needed at The Caste Hotel since last Christmas. It would be the sensible thing to do, of course.

But the thought of working under the eagle eye of Taran's mother, and not daring to say anything untoward to Taran himself for fear of losing her employment and the good reference that would be essential to find another post, filled Catrin with dread. It would be, she thought to herself, like signing away any free choice she might have in the matter of a husband.

'I can walk down,' she murmured.

'Nonsense. Taran will be pleased to take you.' Dad sent an elaborate wink in her direction. 'Very pleased indeed.'

'I wonder if they found the Snowdon Lily,' said Catrin, quickly, trying to head off any further discussion of the matter.

'Taran is a good guide. They'll have as good a chance as any,' replied Dad, drinking his tea in slow satisfaction.

'But he's not the best,' replied Catrin, with a smile, dropping a swift kiss on her father's forehead as she turned to make her way back to the kitchen to leave everything clean and tidy for Mari to take over when she arrived in a few hours. 'And I rather suspect, Dad, that Miss Meredith always demands the best.'

* * *

The sun was beginning to sink low over the sea in a huge orange glow that warmed the tips of the mountains and the edges of the small white clouds sailing serenely above, when Catrin and Taran began to make their descent down the winding track to Llanberis.

The pony plodded steadily along, while the cart rattled away over stones and potholes as went down into the deep shadow of the valley.

I shall probably never see them again, thought Catrin to herself, looking back briefly as the guesthouse disappeared from view in the turn of a bend. Miss Meredith and her brother were booked until Sunday.

By then, Judith had declared, they would have the photograph of the Lily and be on their way back to London, before their competitors could catch up with them. Longer than that, and it would be almost certainly too late.

Catrin looked down towards the lakes stretching down the base of the valley, deep blue in the reflected light from the sky, with the harsh edges of the slate mine scarring the hills on one side mirrored perfectly in the dark stillness of the water.

Always before, she had been glad to get away for a few days from the hustle and bustle of the guesthouse, where her feet scarcely seemed to touch the ground and the smell of cooking never seemed to leave her hair. Much as she loved her time with the climbers and the plant collectors, she always felt herself relax back into herself once she spotted the smoke rising from the cottages of Llanberis.

Then she knew she was on her way back to the peace and quiet of her own home, where she could sleep in her own little whitewashed room, and make just her own breakfast before feeding the hens and settling down to the household tasks, and a cup of tea and a jangle with Nain in the afternoon, before attacking the encroaching weeds in the garden if the rain held off.

But today she felt a strange restlessness going through her, as if she had left something behind in the guesthouse that would haunt her waking hours for many days yet. Many nights, too, perhaps.

Was it the sight of Judith, just a few hours ago, striding down the mountain-side, her skirts swinging jauntily in the afternoon light, and the glow of a day on the mountain on her face that had stirred this unknown longing inside her? Or maybe —

'Fine evening, Catrin,' said Taran beside her.

'Yes, beautiful,' she murmured politely. She had resolved to speak to him as little as possible on this journey, which was not of her choosing, and which made her feel uncomfortable being so close to him without the distraction of companions.

'A beautiful evening made even more lovely by my companion,' said Taran, gallantly. Catrin suppressed a sigh. She was in no mood for any kind of flirtation, and especially not with Taran.

'Do you think Dad will find the lily for Miss Meredith?' she said, quickly.

Taran shrugged. 'I took them to the

place. It wasn't there.'

'It's always been there before,' said Catrin. 'Maybe it was not the right place.'

'I know where the lily is well enough,' returned Taran, loudly. 'Someone must have taken the lily. Such a fuss over a mere flower. Have these rich English people nothing better to do?'

'Miss Meredith has a reason for photographing the lily. She needs it to fund her next expedition,' retorted Catrin, feeling her temper beginning to rise despite herself.

Taran gave a scornful snort. 'Expedition! A woman climbing mountains with no care for her reputation and her dignity. I don't know what her father can be thinking of.'

'Well, I think she is brave and someone to be admired.' Catrin discovered Taran staring at her in astonishment. As he caught her eye, she saw his gaze narrow.

'Perhaps you would like to join her, then.'

'Perhaps I would.'

'Or maybe there is another attraction to be found in her company.'

'I don't know what you mean.'

'Oh, I think you do. This sudden interest in the taking of photographs, don't tell me it came out of thin air.'

'Taran, don't be ridiculous.' Catrin turned on him with barely disguised irritation. 'Just because I show an interest in something doesn't mean . . . ' She paused, finding herself fighting down a blush that came from nowhere. 'Do you think my only interest in life is finding myself a husband?'

'A husband?' Taran scoffed. 'You don't think the likes of Philip Meredith would have any intention of marrying the likes of you, do you, Catrin? His intentions are much baser, I can assure you. And you are a fool to think anything otherwise.'

'I don't think anything about it at all,' snapped Catrin, her temper now well and truly roused. 'And if you think I'm such an idiot, I'm surprised you have any interest in me. I'm quite sure you'll be easily able to find someone more suited to your own perfection.'

She had gone too far. The moment the words were out of her mouth, she knew she had gone too far. She had never before dared to speak her mind when Taran was within hearing, let alone show the edge of her temper.

She bit her lip as the cart began to slow down at the outskirts of the village, where the mock turrets and battlements of the Castle Hotel could be seen peering through the trees. Taran, she discovered, was eyeing her with his brows drawn together and lines of anger tightening his mouth.

Catrin shivered. There was a hard coldness about Taran's anger that frightened her far more than if he had been letting his temper spill over into harsh words.

It was a bottled-up, resentful kind of anger. The kind, she suddenly realised that would grow and grow in silence, feeding on itself until it was beyond anyone's power to control. All of a sudden, all she wanted was to get as far away from him as possible.

'I'll take you home,' he muttered, stiffly.

'Here will do. Thank you,' she returned, leaping down from the seat beside him and reaching for her backpack. Taran was staring into the far distance, an expression of pride and disdain on his face. Despite her dislike of him, she could not leave things like this, Llanberis was too small a community for anyone to live easily with enemies amongst its midst.

Catrin might not wish to marry him, but she had no more of a wish for him to hate her. 'And thank you for bringing me back down,' she said, in warmer tones. 'I'm sure you are right, the lily must no longer be on the mountain.'

'Or awaiting a more worthy finder,' said Taran, his eyes on the carriage drawn up in front of the hotel, its passengers disembarking amidst loud and excited chatter. Catrin followed his gaze. As she watched, a large and cumbersome backpack, very like the one she had seen on Philip as he trudged down the mountainside earlier that day, was lifted out, to loud shouts of, 'take care, you idiots' from more than one of the travellers. A second backpack followed the first.

'Lord Beckinsdale has been expected this past week.' Taran was smug. 'Now there's a real mountaineer for you.'

'A rich one, you mean,' said Catrin.

'A rich one who can pay well, and succeed in his mission,' retorted Taran. 'I'll have more money than you can ever imagine after this.'

Catrin shot him an uneasy glance. Taran wouldn't have deliberately led Judith and Philip to the wrong place, would he? And even if he had, surely he must know that Dad would take them to the correct position to see the lily tomorrow?

But then if Taran had known all along that Lord Beckinsdale was arriving today, his delaying tactics had already deprived Judith of a head start. Now it would be up to the weather and the skill of the guides to determine which of the rivals would achieve their goal first.

And to just what lengths would Taran go, she found herself wondering, uneasily, to ensure his group would reach the lily first? And if Dad was the one leading the rivals —

Catrin swallowed. She may have just made certain once and for all that she would never hear an offer of marriage from Taran, but that also meant he now had nothing to lose as far as her father was concerned.

A breeze stirred across the lake, sending a shower of rain against her face.

'I must go,' she murmured, hastily. The next moment, she was hurrying down the street, away from Taran and the new group of searchers after the Snowdon Lily, and towards the safety of home.

5

For the next two days, the clouds were back down low on the mountains. There was no sign of energetic activity from the group in the Castle Hotel. Taran must know that Dad wouldn't be so foolish as to take his clients up with the mist so thick and the wind gusting so strongly around the peaks, and that he could afford to bide his time.

Catrin watched the clouds swirl around the cliffs of Snowdon as she attacked the weeds in the vegetable patch of the Owen's small cottage. When she walked to the shops in the village she could see the waters of Llanberis lake blown into waves, white with spray, that made it seem as if the sea had found its way this far inland in the night and was straining impatiently at the banks, ready to engulf the entire valley.

As evening began to fall on the second day, the wind lessened. The waters of the lake smoothed back into its usual dark calm, while behind the ruin of Dolbadarn Castle the clouds slowly began to lift. Catrin paused on her way to purchase a few cheap cuts of meat for tonight's stew for herself and Nain and looked up towards the steep cliffs emerging, bit by bit into a stream of afternoon sun.

'Looks to me as if tomorrow will be fine, at last.' Catrin jumped at the voice just behind her.

'And about time, damn it.' A second voice, thinner and more impatient than the first joined the first.

'I'll hurry up that guide fellow, make sure he has no excuses for an early start.'

'He most probably will, Beckinsdale. I'll bet you anything you care to name these fellows are as lazy as they come and will only stir themselves when the sun is set to shine fair all day.'

So they were the mountaineers from

the Castle Hotel! Catrin slowed her pace, pulling out her purse and making a show of counting the coins left inside.

Luckily, they were unlikely to take notice of a local girl out on her duties, and, knowing the usual rich and privileged visitors at the Castle, they would more than likely assume that she spoke not a word of English, anyhow.

'He came highly recommended, and he seems eager enough to lead us to the flower.'

'Eager for the hard cash, you mean. I've no doubt that's where his loyalties really lie.'

What a vile man! Catrin felt her flesh crawl at the cynical draw of his tones. And how unfair if he was the one who was to get the prize for the first photographic image of the Snowdon Lily instead of Judith.

Beckinsdale laughed. 'So paying him well should be a good investment, by your book, Sullivan. And you were the one who begrudged giving him a good fee at all.'

'Fellows like that have no sense of money,' retorted Sullivan. 'And what else can he do with it in this god-forsaken place than drink his brains out. Whatever he might have of them. The sooner we've found this damned flower and are on our way back to London, the better.'

The two men had now stopped, and were admiring the paintings displayed in a shop window. Feeling she could hardly linger any longer without attracting suspicion, Catrin made a show of crossing to the baker's on the opposite side of the street, allowing her to take a quick glance back towards the two.

There was no mistaking which of them was Sullivan. He was tall and thin, with the meanest line of a moustache adorning his long, pale face. She could see from his expression he was finding nothing good to say about the pictures he was viewing.

Sullivan. Wasn't that the name Judith had mentioned? The name of the banker her father had decreed she should marry? The man she had disliked so much?

But if he was the same man, what on earth was he doing here? He didn't seem to have much attachment to the mountains, and even less for the flower they were seeking. So what possible cause could have brought him here? And surely he must know that Judith was in search of the lily, and that Lord Beckinsdale was therefore her rival —

Catrin swallowed. There was a reason for him being there, of course. One very powerful reason: if he was determined Judith should marry him, then what better way to secure the fact than to prevent her from winning the prize for the lily, and the 'hard cash' as he had just put it, to enable her to escape his clutches and take herself off on another climbing expedition. She looked up towards the clearing cloud now retreating bend by bend up towards Peny-Pass.

And Judith was up there, without an

idea of any plot against her. And so was Dad, just as unawares, caught right in the middle of it all . . .

* * *

'Your dad will come out of it well enough,' said Nain, cheerfully, spooning hot stew on to the plates.

'He's a survivor, that one. There aren't many people can put one past Will Owen.'

'I just wish I could warn him, that's all,' sighed Catrin. Her stomach had been in a knot ever since she had overheard the conversation between the two men that afternoon, and the mere thought of eating was making her feel vaguely nauseous.

'A few days' time and you'll be back up there, *cariad*.'

'But by then it might well be too late.'

Nain paused, spoon in mid air. 'You don't really think it can be that serious, do you, Catrin?'

'There's a huge sum of money at stake, Nain.'

'Mmm.' Nain frowned. 'Money can make men do many strange things.'

'I just don't want Dad hurt, that's all, Nain. And he doesn't know about Taran guiding Lord Beckinsdale. And he doesn't know about Mr Sullivan. I'm just sure Mr Sullivan would do anything to stop Miss Meredith from winning that prize. It was bad enough when all those fern collectors were fighting each other, last year. Uncle John said men were stealing each other's backpacks, and taking boots in the night and throwing them over a cliff.'

Nain chuckled. 'And young Rob Jones made a fortune selling dried up bits of bracken as rare Snowdon curling-leafed fern, when anyone with any sense might have known there is no such thing. Not that I'm begrudging the fine wedding he and Meg had, and at least they invited all of Llanberis to share it with them.'

She gazed once more at her granddaughter's worried face. 'But you're right, *cariad*, for most of the visitors it was just the collecting, not the winning of large sums of money.'

She put down the plate in front of her, only half filled. 'Of course, I expect young Guto will be taking himself off to his Aunt Margaret tonight. This is his usual day. He'll be bringing her and her sheep down for the market in Caernarfon the morning.'

Catrin looked up. Guto's Aunt Margaret had worked the farm just under Crib Goch on her own ever since the death of her husband almost twenty years ago. Catrin often walked over to see the old lady when she had a few hours to herself at Uncle John's guesthouse as the farm was only a few minutes' walk away.

'When will he be going?'

'Oh, if you were to make your way to the square in a few minutes' time, I expect you'll see him there, loading up with supplies.'

'Nain — '

'*Duw*, girl. If you're worrying, there's no good you'll be down here. I'll make sure the birds don't start feasting on the beans and Billy Twm and his brothers don't go helping themselves to potatoes when they should be in school, the little rascals. Well? Go on then. What are you waiting for?' She gave a large wink. 'You'll make young Guto a happy man for weeks, if there's nothing else you do. Now get a move on, girl, or you'll be missing him . . . '

Nain was right, of course. Guto could scarcely believe his luck at Catrin's breathless request.

He looked so proud with her sitting beside him all the way through Llanberis and up the mountain road, that Catrin felt a wave of guilt that all she could think of was how slow the journey seemed all of a sudden.

They reached the entrance to Aunt Margaret's farm just as dusk crept in amongst the rocks, sending the crevices into deep shadow, and a touch of cold edged the evening air.

'I'll take you right up there, if you like, Catrin,' said Guto, shyly. 'It won't take long, and Aunt Margaret isn't expecting me for, oh, well, hours, yet.'

'It's all right, Guto. I'll be fine walking. It's only a few minutes, and I'm sure Aunt Margaret has your dinner all ready and waiting.'

'Are you sure you'll be . . . ' Guto swallowed, so clearly torn between disappointing his aunt — who, Catrin was quite sure, really would have dinner cooked and be waiting for his arrival with all the eagerness of a lonely old woman expecting her only nephew — and his anxiety to please his passenger.

'I'll be fine,' said Catrin, gently. 'You've helped me more than I can say already.'

Guto blushed to the roots of his hair, and glowed with the pride of a knight of old rushing in to battle the dragon with his lady's favour fluttering from his lance. He took a deep breath.

'Catrin — '

'I must go, if I wasn't to get up there before dark,' said Catrin, hastily. She wasn't quite sure whether to laugh or cry when he stopped the bold words rising to his lips instantly.

'Of course. Of course. You must hurry, Catrin. I'll watch and make sure you get to the top of the path.'

Catrin gave him a solemn smile. 'Thank you, Guto.' And with that, she escaped up towards the guesthouse as fast as she could.

* * *

'Nonsense, girl. You're imagining things.'

Will Owen stood with his back to the fire and frowned at his daughter. '*Duw*, and it was a shock you gave me, appearing like that out of the dusk. And there was I thinking something had happened to your nain.'

'But Dad — '

'And putting poor Guto to trouble like that! Apart from the fact of driving off alone with a young man, in front of everyone. And just what do you think Taran will make of that?'

'He can make of it what he likes,' retorted Catrin.

'Everyone in Llanberis knows Guto and I have been friends since we were babies, and we're hardly likely to begin eloping now.'

'Catrin!' Dad was looking at her, well and truly shocked. 'I don't want you saying such words, young lady. I don't want you thinking such words. The sooner you are married the better, if those are the things pressing on your mind, if you ask me.'

'I'm sorry, Dad.' Catrin took a deep breath, fighting down her frustration. 'I'm sorry. I didn't mean it like that. I'm just worried about you, that's all.'

'And are you sure it was Richard Sullivan you saw?' demanded Judith. She had been sitting so quietly by the fire, gazing into the depths of the logs, that Catrin had almost forgotten her.

'Lord Beckinsdale called him Sullivan,' she said. 'And you said the description matched that of your fiancé.'

'My never-to-be fiancé, you mean,' said Judith, angrily. 'I know he's backed Lord Beckinsdale's adventures before. It has to be him, Philip, it just has to be him.'

'It doesn't necessarily mean that Father sent him,' said Philip.

'Oh, no. I wouldn't be surprised if Father has no idea of his little scheme at all. Richard knows he doesn't approve of Lord Beckinsdale.' She bared her teeth in a savage kind of a grin. 'At least Father can recognise some fortune-hunters when he sees them.'

'I thought you said you had no money?' demanded Catrin, frowning.

'Catrin!' Will Owen appeared to be convinced his daughter had lost her mind and was capable of voicing every outrageous thought that came into her head, never mind the consequences.

But Judith did not appear offended.

'Oh, I don't. Not until I am thirty. Thirty! What use is a fortune, then? I shall be old and decrepit, and all my joints will ache and I won't be able to get up the smallest hill, let alone a mountain.'

Philip chuckled. 'Let me assure you from experience, Judith, that thirty is not the end of the world.'

'But I can't wait a whole five more years of being penniless,' she retorted.

'Maybe Richard Sullivan can't either, then,' remarked Catrin. She was trying to be sympathetic, but she couldn't help feeling that if she knew someone was leaving her a fortune to be hers for the rest of her life, she wouldn't in the least mind waiting until she was thirty. Forty, even.

'Oh, he won't have to.' Judith turned her attention back to the fire, sunk in gloom. 'My fortune becomes mine immediately once I am married.' She prodded the nearest log with her foot, viciously, causing sparks to fly all around her. 'Not that it will be mine, of course, since the moment I'm married the law says my husband will gain control of everything I have, and I will never have anything that is truly mine, ever again.'

Catrin looked over towards Philip.

'Now don't blame me,' he exclaimed, 'I didn't make the rules. And, personally speaking, I'd be ashamed to insist on controlling my wife's purse-strings like that, as if she were nothing but a child with no sense at all.'

'Really?' Catrin found herself smiling at him.

'Of course, Miss Owen. I'm a rational man, not some power-crazed would-be emperor. What else should I think?' He was smiling back, a wide, generous smile, full of warmth that was making Catrin go tingly all over. Out of the corner of her eye she caught sight of Dad, growing rapidly purple in the face. She could already hear the lecture on 'unashamed flirtation' and 'these artists with their foreign libertine ways' awaiting her at the end of all this.

'So what are you going to do about Taran and Richard Sullivan?' she demanded, as quickly as she could, hoping to distract her father, for a little while, at least.

'Snowdon is a large mountain, there is room enough for us all,' said Dad. 'And Taran will see fair play, just as I will. And that's an end of the matter.'

Across the room, Catrin met Philip's eyes once more, and this time neither of them were smiling. Philip, Catrin could see, had no more faith than she in Taran — or his employers, come to that — having any sense of fair play where money was concerned. But there was nothing either of them could do to persuade Will Owen of the fact.

From where she stood, Catrin could make out the cold light of a full moon, undimmed by cloud, creeping in from behind the curtains.

The only thing they could do, it seemed, was to hope.

6

'I'm coming with you.' Catrin tightened the last lace on her stout walking boots and pushed the old woollen jumper she had borrowed from Uncle John last night, after the others had gone to bed, firmly down into her bulging backpack.

'Don't be ridiculous.' Dad was practically choking over his breakfast. 'Such a thing is quite unseemly.'

'Not as unseemly as Miss Meredith spending all day on the mountains without a chaperone.'

'She has a chaperone in her brother.'

'But he's bound to be left several paces behind with that heavy pack of his, and then he'll be concentrating on taking his photographs. What kind of a chaperone is that?'

Dad eyed her, suspiciously. Catrin smiled.

'I've never heard of such a thing.'

'And besides, Dad, if there are going to be plenty more lady climbers you might start needing me to act as a chaperone for them.' Her smile sweetened. 'You know how people talk.'

'Nonsense.' He frowned at her, not quite so confident now. 'They'll all have their ladies' maids, or whatever.'

'But suppose the ladies' maids fall ill. Or have a fit of the vapours. I mean, ladies' maids don't exactly expect to be dragged up mountains and across narrow ledges with death-defying drops on either side, do they?'

'I — ah, um.' Dad chewed his last piece of bread, considering his response to this argument. Nothing suitable seemed to occur to him. 'But you'll obey everything I tell you,' he added, at last.

'Oh, yes Dad.'

'And no going off in search of lilies on your own, or anything else that takes your fancy.'

'No, Dad.'

'And no, ah, loitering with a certain young man.'

'Dad, I'm coming as a chaperone, such a thought had never crossed my mind.'

'Hrmph.' Will Owen appeared to be building up steam for a bout of parental discipline, but under his daughter's most winning smile he softened. 'Well, just mind you stick to your word,' he muttered, 'or I'll be sending you back without a second warning.'

'Yes, Dad,' said Catrin, demurely.

It was promising to be a perfect day. A few wisps of cloud made their way slowly across the peaks, but apart from that the sun shone out from a clear blue sky.

From the moment the little party set off in the direction of the summit, Catrin knew she was going to enjoy herself.

With Philip burdened down by his photographic equipment, and the rest of them sharing ropes and food and spare bits of clothing, Dad struck an easy pace. After all, they had set off so early even the most dedicated of climbers were scarcely abroad yet, and on a summer's day like this one they had plenty of time until darkness should start to fall.

For a while they followed the well-trodden route to the summit, before branching off to pick their way between boulders and across scree slopes towards the less frequented parts of the mountain.

'At least we seem to have a head start,' said Judith, pausing to peer into the shadows of the mountainsides curving round the lake at the centre of the Snowdon peaks.

'We have the advantage from starting a good way up,' said Dad. 'Lord Beckinsdale's party will have to begin almost from sea level. So we have a great advantage.'

'Good.' Judith glanced back towards her brother, plodding slowly under the cumbersome weight of his backpack. 'But we still have no time to lose.'

'And I suppose that gives me no time to catch my breath?' demanded Philip, resting for a moment, bracing the backpack on a large rock and breathing hard.

'None at all.' And Judith was off once more, following their guide with the lithe step of a mountain goat.

Catrin hesitated. She didn't like to offend a man's pride, but —

'Would you like some water, Mr Meredith?'

'Please.' He grinned at her, a little ruefully. 'This pack was sold to me as a miracle of compactness and lightness it would be possible to take anywhere. I'm afraid I cannot entirely agree.'

'But somewhat easier than pulling a wagon up here?'

He laughed. 'At this moment, I have to confess I have my doubts.' He took a drink. 'I just hope this lily makes its appearance today, that is all. Then I can go back down to flat ground and contemplate how I can take photographs without dragging everything I could possibly need on my back.' He handed back the water bottle. 'Although I have to confess it is very beautiful. I might just be tempted up again to take a few landscapes from up here.'

'Good,' said Catrin.

'Well, I'm glad that pleases you, that should give me the energy for the rest of the day.'

'I didn't mean — What I meant was — ' She frowned at him as severely as she knew how. 'What I meant was, I'm glad you like the mountains and want to photograph them. And I didn't mean anything else.'

'I believe you.' He straightened up, steadying himself with his stout walking cane. 'Especially with your father looking as if he would like to horsewhip me from here to kingdom come.'

Catrin swung round, to find Dad was indeed watching them closely. 'Although he might consider I'm in no position to get up to no good at this present time, however great the temptation.'

'I should hope not,' returned Catrin. 'I thought you were supposed to be concentrating on photographing a certain lily?'

'Mmm. I can see that one day that sister of mine will get me into one scrape too far, one of these days,' he grumbled to himself, with a wink in Catrin's direction, as he set out once more on his laborious uphill journey. 'I can see I shall have to deal with that once I get down from here, too.'

Catrin smiled, and made her way up to join the others.

'No loitering,' said Dad, gruffly, as she reached them.

'I merely gave the man a drop of water. You can hardly expect me to leave my Christian compassion behind, do you?'

'Hrmph,' said Dad, eyeing her closely. Fortunately, Judith was growing impatient at yet a further delay in proceedings. 'I'll deal with you later, my girl,' he muttered, making his way in front of the party once more.

It was almost noon by the time they reached the steep cliffs where the rare specimens found their hiding places.

'Where now?' demanded Judith, peering up at the smooth slopes of rock.

'On that ledge, just to your right,' said Dad, lifting the coil of rope from his body. 'I take it you have undertaken rock-climbing before, Miss?'

'Of course.' Judith was indignant. 'And in far higher places than this.'

'Good. I'll go up first and secure the rope. Then the rest of you can follow.' He tied one end of the rope around his waist with a practised movement, handing the rest to Catrin. 'And you don't go anywhere until my daughter tells you to. Understand?'

'Of course, Mr Owen.'

'Just so long as that is understood. I've done my share of carrying men with broken limbs down to safety for this season. I've no intention of having to take anyone down from up here.'

He secured the rope and set off, moving carefully from one foothold to another, with Catrin letting out the rope as it was needed.

'I'm not looking forward to that with that weight on my back,' said Philip, resting the pack against the rock face and rubbing his shoulders.

'You have to. How else are you going to photograph the lily?'

'I didn't say I wouldn't, Judith. I just said I didn't like the idea.' He looked around him, frowning. 'I thought we were going to the same place we went before.'

'With Taran, you mean?' asked Catrin.

'Yes. It looks more or less the same. But I could have sworn it was a little farther over towards those dark cliffs over there.'

'He must have been mistaken, then,' said Judith, dismissing the matter.

'He was recommended as an experienced guide,' replied Philip.

'Well, guides can make mistakes.'

'Perhaps.' He met Catrin's eye. 'It's possible.'

'Taran has been bringing botanists here for years,' said Catrin, slowly. 'He couldn't make a mistake like that.'

'You mean, he took us to the wrong place deliberately?' Judith frowned at her. 'What on earth for?'

'To delay us, I should imagine. Don't you agree, Miss Owen?'

Catrin nodded, wordlessly.

'Well, the more fool him.' Judith took a drink from her water bottle. 'We still got here first, before Richard could spoil it for us.'

'But why would he? Richard hadn't arrived when Taran brought us up here, Judith. He'd have no cause to prevent us finding the lily, unless — ' He gave a glance in Catrin's direction, and took to clearing his throat as if overcome by a sudden cold.

'Unless Mr Sullivan — or Lord Beckinsdale — had already paid him to prevent you from photographing the Snowdon Lily,' Catrin continued for him.

'That sounds like one of Richard's tricks. But he's wasted his money, in this case.'

Catrin looked up towards her father, who had now reached the top of the climb and was manoeuvring himself on to the ledge. Cold sweat, that had nothing to do with the exertions of the day, began to trickle down her spine. She found Philip watching her.

'You don't think Taran would do anything foolish, do you?' he asked, his voice too low for his sister to hear.

'I don't know. I can't imagine any guide on the mountains wishing to harm the lily, and, besides, none of the other guides would ever let him work again.'

'But you think it might be possible?'

'If there was money enough.' Catrin sighed. 'Taran has always been ambitious. I fear if he thought he could ingratiate himself with rich and powerful men . . . well then I'm afraid he might be capable of anything.'

Dad had vanished. Taran couldn't

have done anything, she told herself. He couldn't. Each specimen of the lily was so rare, the loss of just one little colony might mean it vanishing from the mountain all together.

No guide with any sense would destroy their own livelihood, and the lily was such an attraction for visitors and botanists alike, and could not be found without the assistance of a guide.

But if Taran was planning a life away from the mountains . . .

Catrin frowned to herself. He had once talked of becoming a gamekeeper to a rich man's estate, she remembered. She had taken it as boasting and had quite put it out of her mind. But Lord Beckinsdale was undoubtedly rich, and most probably in possession of a very large estate somewhere in England. It was with relief she saw Dad leaning over the edge of the rock once more.

'Are you ready for me?' Judith called up, impatient as ever.

'No.' At the hollowness of his voice, Catrin's heart sank.

‘In a few moments, then?’

‘No. There is no point in coming up here at all.’ Dad was already swinging himself over the ledge and back on to the first foothold.

‘No point? Of course there’s a point. It’s what we’ve come to see.’

‘Not now it isn’t. There’s nothing to see.’

‘Nothing?’ Judith was incredulous. Philip made his way towards her and put a comforting hand on her arm. ‘How can there be nothing? You said this is the place.’

‘Oh, it’s the place, all right,’ returned Dad, grimly. ‘But you won’t be finding the Snowdon Lily here. It’s gone. Every last flower, leaf and stem of it has disappeared completely. There will be no photographing of the Snowdon Lily today.’

7

'Richard couldn't have done this. He couldn't.' Judith had her head in her hands, her voice choked with tears.

'I don't imagine he did it personally,' said Philip. 'These are the sort of occasions henchmen are hired for.'

'I never thought he'd go so far to stop me. He's a brute. A complete brute. And I'll never marry him now, whatever happens. I'd rather go into a convent.'

Catrin suppressed a smile at the thought of the headstrong Judith Meredith lasting so much as a day amongst the company of nuns. From the hand discreetly covering his mouth, it seemed that Philip felt much the same.

'And I'll not be letting this rest.' Will Owen was still pale with fury at the desecration. 'The Royal Cambrian Society shall be hearing of this.'

'But you won't be able to prove who did take the lily, Dad. And if you accuse Lord Beckinsdale, won't he just say that you were the one who destroyed it? And who will listen to you and me if there is a lord in the case.'

'That's remarkably cynical for one so young,' said Philip, brows raised.

'But it's true, though, isn't it?'

'Unfortunately, yes. And I'm afraid Judith and I won't carry any more weight, either.'

'You mean, you're just going to let him get away with it?' Judith dashed the tears from her eyes and glared at her companions. 'Well I'm not. I don't care what it takes, I shall expose him for what he is, if it's the last thing I do.'

'We'd better get down to the guesthouse,' said Philip, quietly. 'We've taken up enough of Mr Owen's time as it is.'

'But there must be another site. More than one.' Judith turned pleadingly to Will Owen. 'There has to be.'

Catrin glanced at her father's face,

but it was set in stone.

'Not that I know of,' he replied. 'Nothing to be done about it, Miss.'

'So they'll win the prize.' Judith was white.

'Unless another party found the lily first, I'm afraid so, Miss.'

'Well, this is not going to be the end of this. I don't care what any of you say, I'm not going to let this be the end of this.' And with that, Judith hoisted her backpack on to her shoulders, and set off at a rapid pace towards the main path.

'Judith — ' Philip watched the retreating figure with exasperation, and more than a little concern. 'Damn this pack.'

'I'll go with her.' Catrin slid her own pack on to her shoulders. 'I'll make sure she doesn't hurt herself, or do anything foolish.' And before Dad could open his mouth to protest, she was picking her way between the boulders in pursuit of the crimson bonnet retreating into the distance.

* * *

Judith had reached the main path by the time Catrin caught up with her. The sun had reached the centre of the mountain by now, warming the steady stream of visitors and their guides making the most of the break in the weather and trudging their way towards the summit.

'I'm going to see,' said Judith, looking upwards to where the path flattened out on the ridge before making its final ascent. 'I'll be able to see all the way down the path to Llanberis. I'm going to see if it was them.'

'It might have happened last night. Or maybe they camped on top and were here early this morning. Besides, with all the other climbers, how will you make them out?'

'Oh, I'll make them out. I know I will.'

'The lily has gone, Judith. What does it matter who took it?'

'It matters to me,' said Judith, a dangerous glint in her eyes. 'It certainly matters to me.'

'I'm glad to hear it.' Both young women jumped at the voice drifting down towards them. Looking up, they discovered a thin figure perched on a rock just above them.

'Richard!' Catrin looked in alarm as her companion raised her walking cane, apparently with every intention of dispatching the thin young man smiling down at them in unmistakable triumph.

'Delighted to see you, too, my dear,' he replied. 'And your pretty little companion. A definite improvement on that brother of yours.'

'I knew it was you behind this. I knew it!'

'Surely a man can enjoy a peaceful walk with his guide?' returned Richard. 'It seems to be a popular pastime on this beautiful day.'

'The lily. You destroyed the lily, Richard.'

'Nonsense, my dear. You need to be a

little wiser in hiring your guide. Haven't you heard there are charlatans no end purporting to know the mountain, when most of them have only seen the paths in a common guidebook themselves, and many of those are unable to read what is written.'

The thin lips parted into a cold laugh. 'I have had a good hour or two's entertainment up here watching you and your so-called guide. He took you to quite the wrong place, my dear, I can assure you.'

'Liar!'

'Well, you are free to call me whatever name you wish now, although I wouldn't advise it once we are married.'

'I'm never going to marry you, Richard. Never.'

'And what other choice, exactly, will you have?' He gave an unpleasant sneer. 'Once the papers get hold of the story of your failure here, you will be quite the laughing stock. I can't imagine anyone wishing to back your little adventures now, my dear, for fear of being laughed at themselves. Quite a sad end to your little foolishness, my dear Judith. Abysmal failure. Well, your luck couldn't hold out forever, you know.'

He rose to his feet. 'And now, my dear, may I suggest that I escort you back to my hotel? That guesthouse of yours is quite unsuitable for my future wife, and that way we can travel back to London together. You know that will please your father and enable him to overlook this little adventure.'

'With the photograph of the lily, you mean?' Judith's eyes had narrowed. Catrin gave a quick glance back along the route they had come. There was no sign of Dad or Philip, it was just her and Judith on her own, and heaven knows what the stubborn young woman next to her was planning now.

Richard Sullivan laughed. 'I'm flattered, Judith. You would actually consider riding back with me on the off-chance of being able to get those delicate hands of yours on the glass plates of the Snowdon Lily.'

'I'm not a thief.'

'No. But I wouldn't put a small accident occurring on our journey back past your capabilities.' Judith bit her lip. 'Yes, I thought so. But there's no need for your touching concern, my dear. I took the precaution of securing the services of more than one guide. The photographs of the lily are safely half way down to Llanberis as we speak, and I've no doubt will be in the carriage and on the way to the London train with Lord Beckinsdale before nightfall, even if I don't get back down there in time to join them.'

He gave a bleak smile as he moved his way down towards them. 'So really, my dear, you have no choice but to accompany me back to the safety of your father's house.'

'Prison, you mean,' muttered Judith under her breath, looking suddenly forlorn. Catrin quietly took her hand and squeezed it, reassuringly. She felt the pressure returned.

Dad must arrive soon! And meanwhile, she wasn't going to let this horrible man drag her new friend away. Both she and Judith were fit and strong, surely between them —

Catrin froze. Behind Richard Sullivan a new figure had risen to his feet, grinning widely. She swallowed.

'Oh congratulations, Richard,' Judith's voice was a whiplash. 'A hired thug to do your dirty work. Very impressive.'

'Come now, Judith, be reasonable.' The two men had reached them by now. 'It really will be the best for you.'

'Leave us alone, Taran.' Catrin stepped farther in front of her companion. 'You've got what you want, haven't you? Now leave us alone.'

'Not quite everything I want,' he returned.

'Oh, don't be a fool.' She stepped away, pulling Judith with her, back towards the shelter of the path. From the corner of her eye she could see a new group of climbers making their way up towards them. 'You can hardly drag us off by our hair.'

As Taran reached forward, she dodged sideways. She was aware of him missing her arm, and the *thwack* of Judith's walking stick coming down hard.

'Don't you dare,' said Judith. 'Don't you dare touch my friend! Now turn around and skulk your way back to your kennels, both of you.'

Taran was rubbing his hand, cursing her under his breath, dodging from one foot to the other attempting to find a way under Judith's ready weapon.

'Taran!' Catrin let out a silent sigh of relief. At last, Dad had caught up with them. At least now they stood a chance. 'Taran, what are you thinking of? Have you gone entirely mad?' Catrin could have laughed at the look of foolish dismay travelling over Taran's face.

'Ah, the guide.' Richard eyed the newcomer with a look of cool disdain. 'The guide who cannot remember where he has left the Snowdon Lily.

Not one I would wish to trust to care for my fiancée. I shall be taking Miss Meredith back to safety, with a guide who really does know his way around Snowdon.'

'Taran?' Dad was frowning. He seemed scarcely to have heard Richard Sullivan's insults. Catrin could see his eyes were fixed on Taran's hands. As she followed his gaze, she could see the earth ingrained in the younger man's hands and under his fingernails. 'I hope you had nothing to do with the destruction of the Snowdon Lily, Taran. Not for all the money in the world.'

'Such a fuss over a plant.' Taran had flushed bright red and could not meet the older man's eyes. 'A plant will grow again.'

'Not if every last part of it is destroyed,' said Dad. 'Take the flower, yes, if you must. But not the plant, roots and all. If this is true, Taran, then you are a disgrace to us all, and not fit to be a guide.'

Taran shrugged. 'I've better things to

do than stay here wandering up and down dirt tracks,' he said. 'I shall never need to work as a guide again.'

'Leave him, Dad,' said Catrin, hastily. 'Let him go. Taran has made his choice. Just let him go.'

'We're wasting time.' Richard Sullivan was growing impatient. 'Come on, Judith, the photographs will be well on their way by now. I'm sure you'll want to be there when they are presented to the Royal Cambrian Society.'

'Leave her alone,' said Dad, loudly. 'The young lady is in my care, and she is not going to be forced into going anywhere against her wishes.'

Catrin caught the movement from the corner of her eye. She glimpsed Taran, his face white with fury and humiliation, pushing forward to grasp Judith, striking Will Owen out of his way.

For a moment the two men struggled, then there was a sickening crash as Dad was flung sideways and down to the hard rocks of the path, where he lay still.

8

'Dad!' Catrin was at his side in a moment. A trickle of blood ran from Will Owen's forehead, and he did not move at her call. Taran looked on, white-faced and uncertain at his fellow guide lying prostrate on the ground. 'Help him, can't you,' said Catrin, anger spilling through her fear. 'You can't just leave him, up here, Taran. No guide could ever leave an injured man this high on Snowdon.'

'You fool,' Richard Sullivan surveyed the catastrophe with nothing more than irritation. 'I said, no attracting attention to ourselves. Judith, you will follow me to the Castle Hotel. As it appears you have no guide now, you really have no choice.' He gave a curt nod to Taran. 'Make sure she comes with you.' And with that, he took his long legs up the path towards the ridge, where the path met up with the route down to Llanberis.

'Don't you dare.' Judith had her walking cane at the ready as Taran approached her, bristling with the blind fury of a trapped animal. Even Taran paused, clearly remembering the way that very same stick had rapped him smartly on the knuckles. No-one could possibly mistake Judith for a young lady suffering a fit of the vapours, she meant business, and Taran hovering from one foot to another, was not one to forget it.

'That will do.' Catrin looked up quickly as Philip, magically unencumbered by his heavy pack, leapt down from the rocks behind them and went to stand beside his sister.

At the sound of his voice, Richard Sullivan paused, and turned back. 'Judith will stay with me,' Philip was saying calmly. 'And I shall ensure that my father hears the truth about what happened here today, Sullivan. I very much doubt he would wish a cheat and a potential murderer as a son-in-law.'

'Do as you please, Meredith.' Richard called back, coldly. 'I've no doubt he will not object to the gallant winner of the first photograph of the Snowdon Lily adding his fame and fortune to your family. Such a pity that a loser of such a prize should not see fit to congratulate the winner, but take to shouting 'cheat' instead.'

'Damn the man!' Philip appeared to be about to take off after him and settle the matter once and for all. But instead, he turned to help Catrin. 'Is your father badly hurt, Miss Owen?'

'I don't know. He seems to have taken a blow to the head, I don't like to move him. His pulse is steady and he is breathing normally. I think he is just unconscious.' She straightened up, and peered down the path towards the lake to where the two guides of the next group of climbers were hurrying towards them. 'Help will be here in a moment. Please don't stay if you want to go after Mr Sullivan.'

'Certainly not. The man's not worth

the trouble, eh, Judith?'

'Except that he's right about Father being impressed by the prize,' said Judith gloomily.

'We'll cross that bridge when we come to it. Meanwhile, we need to get Catrin's father down to safety.' He shot a scowl over towards Taran, who was hesitating, clearly torn between his employer, and the tattered remains of loyalty to Will Owen. 'Well? Are you going to help us?'

Taran flushed under the scorn in the other man's voice. He glanced up to Richard, who had now reached the ridge, and was disappearing over to the other side, and then back to the arriving guides, now just a few paces away down the path.

'Catrin.' He looked at her with a mixture of sullenness and pleading. 'I didn't mean this to happen, Catrin. All I wanted was the makings of a better life. For you, Catrin. It was all for you.'

Judith gave a loud snort at this,

causing Taran to flush an even deeper shade.

Catrin eyed him, squarely. ‘I never asked you for such a thing, Taran,’ she returned, firmly. ‘I told you as plain as I knew how that I never wished to marry you. You’ve insulted me and threatened me to try and get me to bend to your wishes. And now you’ve put my father’s life in danger. I want nothing more than to never have to set eyes on you again.’

There was a moment’s silence, while Taran stood there, turning first white and then red. Next to Caitlin, Will Owen was beginning to stir.

With a groan, he pulled himself up to a sitting position, leaning heavily against the rock, one hand on the wound on his forehead, his eyes fixing on the young man before him.

Taran swallowed. The two guides had now reached the little group. From the expressions on their faces as they eyed Taran, it was quite clear they had seen everything that had taken place. This time Taran's face was as grey as the rock that surrounded him.

The next moment, he had turned, and was racing up the path towards his vanishing master with all the recklessness of a man who no longer cared what should happen to him.

⋆ ⋆ ⋆

'Well, it could be worse.' Rhys Evans finished his inspection of Dad's head wound, and nodded to Catrin to continue applying the bandage. 'At least I can feel no fracture of the skull.'

'You surprise me,' muttered Will Owen, ruefully. 'If you ask me, an entire mountain fell on my head just now.'

'It'll serve to keep you off the beer for a while,' returned Rhys, with a grin. He became serious once more. 'I'm not so happy about those ribs, though, Will, to be honest with you. I'd say you've at least one that's badly bruised, if not cracked. But at least it doesn't appear to be broken, so there will be no sharp pieces there to start penetrating your lungs.'

'Well, thank Heavens for small mercies.' Dad pulled himself to his feet as Catrin finished the bandaging, wincing at the pain in his ribs. 'Thirty years I've been up and down Snowdon, blizzards, thunderstorms and all, without a scratch on me until that fool Taran begins thinking of his own fortune rather than the welfare of the mountain.'

He gave Catrin a brief smile. 'And there I was, about to send you kicking and screaming down the aisle with him.'

'Nonsense, Dad. You'd never have been able to send me screaming anywhere, when it came to it. And, besides, it doesn't matter now. All that matters is getting you safely off this mountain.'

'*Duw*, girl, don't be worrying about me. All I need is a bit of steadying and I'll be making my way down in no time.'

'Not on your own, you're not,' replied Rhys. 'We've been on many a rescue together up here, Will, and I can't be losing your knowledge of the mountain now. I'm staying with you until I see you safely down at your brother's guesthouse and in front of the fire with a good hot toddy in your hands.'

'Hrmmph,' said Dad. But he didn't argue. The little group of walkers had readily agreed to sacrifice the services of one of their guides for the rest of the day, with an injured man to get down to safety, and had gone on ahead to the summit leaving Rhys Evans behind.

'I'll go and fetch my backpack,' said Philip, quietly, leaving a dejected Judith staring down towards the lake below.

'No, no.' Will Owen frowned at him. 'You leave it where you left it young man. No point in bringing it back here, with all that weight dragging you down.' Philip blinked.

'I'm afraid I must. That is a very expensive piece of equipment, sir. I'm certain I can manage to carry it and assist you down to the guesthouse.'

'Assist?' Dad's eyes were bright under the bandage. 'Who said anything about assisting? I can manage with Rhys here. You've not time to waste if you don't want to be missing the light.'

'The light?' Philip clearly believed the older man had turned delirious.

'That's what you need, isn't it? Good light for the photographing of the lily.'

'But the lily has gone, sir,' said Philip, gently.

Dad chuckled. 'It's quite all right, young man. My memory is as good as ever it was, despite the thunder in my head. A lily was gone. You don't think it's the only one, do you?'

'You mean, there's another?' Judith looked up, the light back in her eyes.

'Of course.'

'But we'll never be able to find it without your help,' protested Philip, 'and, besides, the photograph will be on its way to London in a few hours, so there really is no point.'

‘I’m sure Miss Meredith isn’t one to give in so quickly,’ returned Dad.

‘I’m afraid Philip is right about the photograph. The prize was for the first one to reach the Royal Cambrian Society in London.’

‘Accidents happen,’ said Will, manoeuvring himself carefully upright. ‘And it’s a long road back through the mountains to the train for your Mr Sullivan’s coach to rattle through.’

‘But we couldn’t insist on you leading us, Mr Owen — ’

‘My dear Philip, I’m not intending to lead you anywhere. Catrin knows the place well enough.’

Catrin frowned at him. ‘I’m not leaving you, Dad.’

‘Nonsense. I’m in the best hands with Rhys, and we’ll be down in a few hours.’

‘And besides . . . ’ She gave a quick glance towards Judith. She could not bear the thought of disappointment back in those eyes, but all the same . . .

‘Oh, I think we can make an

exception, just this once,' said Dad. 'Don't you agree, Rhys?'

'An exception to what?' demanded Judith.

'No-one knows where these lilies are,' explained Catrin. 'Only the most experienced guides, and they never take visitors to see them. So that, whatever happens, a few of the flowers will always survive.'

'But Taran — ' Philip frowned at them.

'Taran was considered still too young,' said Dad. 'Young men can be distracted by all kinds of things. Even the best of them.' His eyes sharpened. 'And let me warn you, both of you, that Catrin will show you where these lilies flower only on condition that neither of you ever breathe a word of it. You must swear that the photograph was taken at the place Taran destroyed the flowers.'

'You mean, leave ourselves open to accusations of being the destroyers?' said Philip.

'Well, for that, you will have to trust

us.' Dad smiled. 'It is late in the season, a few more days and the lily's flowers will be over. By next summer I'm sure you'll find a few lilies have found their way to that very place. And no-one need ever know.'

'Apart from Richard,' muttered Judith.

'Oh, I think we can deal with your Richard,' said Dad.

Catrin shot him an anxious glance. There weren't many times when Dad took such matters in a personal light, but Richard Sullivan's corruption of Taran was one he appeared to have taken to heart. She just hoped he wouldn't do anything foolish. Not that Dad would listen to reason, once he had got an idea in his head, cracked ribs or not.

'Well — ' Philip glanced at Catrin. 'Are you sure about this?'

Catrin nodded. 'Even if there is just the smallest chance, surely we have to take it.'

'Agreed,' said Judith, already on her

feet and prepared for action.

Catrin took a deep breath. The hiding place for the most secret of lilies was not an easy one to reach, and it was not a task she had ever attempted on her own. But now it would all be up to her.

'You take care, Dad,' she said, giving her father a kiss on the cheek.

'And you make sure you are home before nightfall, my girl,' he returned, his old severity back in his voice. Catrin smiled.

9

Catrin paused, catching her breath before she pulled herself up through the next collection of boulders beneath the high cliffs of the mountain above. Below, she could just make out the two tiny figures making their way along the far end of the lake and back down towards the warmth and safety of the guesthouse at Pen-y-Pass.

'It looks as if your father is making his way down without too many problems, Catrin.' She smiled down at Philip, who was pulling himself up to join her.

'I hope so,' she said. She looked at him with a serious gaze. 'Thank you,' she added. 'I don't know what we would have done if you hadn't risked leaving your photography equipment and arrived so fast.'

'Ah well, call it a pleasure. I never

was over-fond of Rich Sullivan. Rather too much of the bully about him.' Philip grinned. 'I dare say our father believed he was the firm hand needed to keep Judith in order, but a little too firm, in my opinion. Of the stifling variety.' His eyes met hers. 'I rather think your father had much the same ideal, concerning husbands.'

'He meant well,' returned Catrin.

'Although he might have consulted your wishes first?'

She sighed. 'I think he sees me as far as too young and inexperienced to make my own decisions on such a weighty matter.'

'And are you?' There was a question in his eyes, as well as in his voice. Catrin felt her gaze flicker, moving from the intensity of his look to his sister pulling herself easily up behind him, scarcely breathing harder than usual.

'Have you seen the view from up here?' Judith's face was shining with excitement. 'Isn't it perfectly heavenly?'

'Yes,' said Catrin. Just for a moment,

her eyes travelled back to rest on those of Philip. She had answered a question, but, for the life of her, she could not have said which one. Or maybe it was both.

'What are you grinning at, like a monkey?' demanded Judith of her brother.

'Oh, nothing,' he replied. Catrin turned and reached for the next handhold, feeling that the more she concentrated on the task at hand the better. The last thing she needed up amongst these unfamiliar cliffs was any kind of distraction.

Judith had already forgotten Philip. 'It is far now, Catrin?'

'Just above, on the ledge past that next overhand of rock. We should be there in a few minutes.'

'Good.' Judith had turned, and was gazing back over the wild stretch of mountainside around them. 'At least we won't lose the light.'

'No.' Catrin carefully kept her tone even. 'But we need to hurry. The wind is getting up again.'

She knew all too well how fast the weather could change on the mountain, and with the ominous stirring of the grasses and the tiny alpine flowers sheltering between rocks growing stronger and more frequent in the last hour of their climb, she had a feeling deep in her belly that they had no time to lose.

The wind had made one of its swift about-turns of direction, no longer bringing in the breeze hurtling in from the sea, ready to disperse its fluffy white clouds as they hit the mountainsides. With the wind now coming from the heart of the high ranges of Snowdonia, the danger of cloud building up around them had increased alarmingly.

Catrin tried not to think too much of the consequences of mist rolling in around them, blotting out the route back to well-marked path down to safety. She was in an unfamiliar part of the mountain without the small landmarks of stones at the side of the path and the crossing of streams to guide her down.

The three climbed quickly up through the large grey boulders, thrown down the steep mountainside as if carelessly discarded by a giant's hand. Catrin shivered a little as the first wisp of cloud swirled around them, before drifting upwards towards the summit. Their footstep echoed hollowly amongst the rocks around them, accompanied every now and then by the roll of small stones dislodged by their boots and sent scurrying down towards the valley floor far below.

'Eerie, eh?' Philip was looking around him, as if catching some of her unease.

'It always seems so away from the main paths,' said Catrin. 'This is where Snowdon is still truly wild.'

'And so do you believe that King Arthur is hidden up here, waiting for the day he will return?'

Catrin smiled. 'Who knows?'

'King Arthur is up here?' Judith peered around her as another rush of cloud swept around them to vanish almost immediately, her usual confidence dented with a touch of unease.

'So says the legend,' said Catrin. She had never experienced the fearless Judith to be so susceptible to the atmosphere of the mountain. 'The story goes that this was the site of King Arthur's last battle. He is supposed to have been rowed across the lake to a cave hidden up here beneath the summit of the mountain.'

'So if you find a large bell, Judith, take care not to make it ring.'

'Nonsense.' Judith straightened her shoulders, determinedly. 'A story is a story. It's only superstition.'

'Like the *Brenin Llwyd*,' murmured Catrin to herself.

'Like who?' demanded Philip.

'Oh, nothing.' She had no wish to think of the Grey King sweeping down on the mountains in the mist to chase the unwelcome to their door at the foot of his domain. She might not be a stranger to the mountains, but she was revealing the last hidden place of the Snowdon Lily, and Catrin didn't feel entirely confident that she wouldn't be included, should the ancient spirits of the mountain be stirred into anger.

They had reached the final ledge. Just above them rose a sheer stretch of rock, seemingly devoid of any kind of hold on its smooth surface.

'Is that it?' demanded Judith.

'Yes. It's not impossible if you know how,' replied Catrin.

'I should hope not,' said Philip, eyeing the smooth surface dubiously.

'I'll go up first and secure the rope. That will make it easier for you to come up with your backpack.' She hesitated a moment, not quite sure how to proceed. 'Do you wish to follow me?' she asked Judith.

Judith frowned. 'Is there room up there for the three of us.' She saw Catrin bite her lip, uncertain how to reply. 'In other words, no.'

'If I secure the rope, I can come

down as soon as your brother is in position . . . '

'No.' Judith shook her head, decisively. 'If we are going to get down tonight and get the photographs to London we need to do this as quickly as possible.' She smiled a faintly rueful smile. 'I would love to see the lily, of course I would. But there will be other times for that. At this moment, time is of the essence.'

Catrin let out a silent breath of relief. She knew she could not have prevented Judith from making the climb if she had insisted, and she understood just how much Miss Meredith's practical side had cost her.

'I will show you. Whatever you wish, I promise,' she said. Judith smiled, the determination back in her face.

'I'll hold you to that, Catrin,' she said. 'Well? What are you waiting for? My feet are wet, and I could eat a horse. The sooner you two get up there the sooner we can get back down again.'

Catrin glanced at Philip. 'Ready?'

He gave a wry grin. 'As I'll ever be. Remind me to teach you the rudiments of photography, Judith, so I can safely send you up rock faces next time.'

'Done,' said Judith. 'I'll hold you to that. Not that he will,' she added. 'Don't take any notice of him, Catrin. Philip is having the time of his life. He just likes to make a fuss.'

'Fuss?' A humorous smile was playing around his lips. 'Just remind me never to leave the comfort of my club next time my sister comes asking just a little favour. Come on then, let's get this over with.'

The climb was even harder than Catrin remembered it. She braced herself against the rock, feeling the rope around her waist pressing into her, as she felt for one handhold and then the next, kicking the folds of her skirt out of the way to allow her boots to grip the shallow cavities in the rock.

Her arms ached, and her legs ached, while the white mist swirling in around her grew thicker and more frequent, enveloping her in a cold white world in which all sound was muffled, and even Judith's anxious voice seemed like a world away. She paused, laying her burning face against the damp coolness of the rock.

'I must be mad,' she thought to herself. But then the vision of Taran, his hands stained with his destruction of the lily, wrestling with Dad and flinging him to the ground swam in front of her eyes, along with the tall, thin figure of Richard Sullivan smiling in triumph as he vanished over the ridge to make the journey back down to Llanberis.

She felt her lips tightened in determination. She didn't care what it took, she was going to give Judith the only chance she could to win the prize and escape Richard Sullivan's clutches. Dad was right, anything could happen on the long journey back to London.

Catrin took a deep breath and steeled herself to take the last few movements up until her fingers reached over the lip of the rock on to the flat surface of the ledge, and with one last effort she pulled herself over to lie there, panting, feeling the sweat pouring down her back inside her dress, her lungs fit to burst.

'Catrin?' Philip sounded anxious. As well he might, given her undignified exit over the edge of the rock. Any other time and she would have blushed with humiliation, not to mention the indecent amount of stocking she had revealed to the world in her scramble to safety. Now she simply wriggled herself upright.

'I'm all right,' she called. 'Just give me a moment to secure the rope.' Abandoning dignity to the winds, she crawled her way to the back of the ledge. The metal spike was still there from the last time Dad had been to check the lily. She secured the rope firmly around the spike, anchoring it with the extra security of a large rock. Then she made her way back to the edge once more. 'You can begin now,' she called. 'Just take it slowly.'

'Slowly? A snail has nothing on me,' Philip called back, dryly.

She laughed.

'As long as you make some progress,' she returned, taking hold of the rope, bracing it round her waist to take the slack as he began to climb. Despite the anchor of the spike and the rock, heaven help them both if he should fall, she thought to herself. She would barely be able to hold the weight of a grown man, while with the addition of the heavy pack — she shut her mind to the possibility.

It was all too easy for her imagination to run forwards to find the rope slipping away from her, and the figure below her tumbling inevitably to his doom on the sharp rocks below. Catrin took a deep breath and hung on grimly.

Fortunately, Philip was sure-footed as he was strong. Furthermore, she discovered, he was not foolhardy and made his way slowly and patiently, rather than attempting to show off his prowess to the two young women anxiously watching his every move. Catrin pulled in the rope and climbed, securing it carefully each time, in case he should slip.

Slowly, foothold-by-foothold, he made his way towards her, until with one last heave, she grasped his wrist and helped him in the final undignified scramble over the edge.

'Never again,' he groaned, breathlessly, as she helped him off with the heavy pack.

'Really?'

'Yes really.' He wiped his brow with his sleeve. 'I can see you don't believe me, Miss Owen.'

Catrin smiled as she began to release the second strap. 'Not a bit of it, Mr Meredith. I think Judith is right: you're enjoying every moment of this.'

'Only the company,' he retorted. She blinked, suddenly aware that the two of them were crouched as close together as they could be, and so practically entwined that Dad, should he ever hear of such a thing, would never let her hear the last of it. She found Philip scrutinising her face. 'You're right, Catrin, this is not the time, or the place.'

'Not exactly,' she returned, but without severity. He smiled, pulling away stray strands of hair caught in her mouth in the effort of holding the tope.

'Not at all,' he replied softly, bending forward so that his lips met hers.

'Philip!' It was Judith's call that had him drawing away from her in a moment, a look of regret on his face.

'I'm quite safe,' he called back.

'Well hurry up. There's a lot more cloud making its way in this direction.'

He sighed. 'I'd quite forgotten the lily.' He reached for his backpack. 'I was far too busy trying to get my face slapped.'

'Were you?' said Catrin, her eyes on his face. She should look severe, she decided. Be shocked and outraged that a man she barely knew should be taking such liberties, and when she was stuck up on a narrow ledge and could scarcely move for fear of toppling back over the edge. But despite her resolution, she found her mouth curling into a smile.

Philip grinned. 'I'm tempted to forget this dratted flower,' he murmured, edging himself closer to her once more.

'Oh no you're not.' Catrin's practical side was reasserting itself, assisted by a racing cloud, much larger and denser than any that had passed them by before, enveloping them briefly in its white softness, so that they could scarcely make out each other's faces.

She grasped his hand. 'Come on, it's over here. You're going to take this photograph, and then I'm going to get you and your sister safely back down off this mountain.'

'A masterful woman.' She could hear the laughter warm in his voice.

'Look! There it is,' said Catrin, hastily. He crawled up to join her. 'And there's one still in bloom. Isn't it beautiful?'

'That's it?' Philip couldn't quite hide

his dismay. 'You mean, that is what all the fuss is about? It's tiny!'

'Of course it's tiny. It's an alpine flower. That's how they survive in places like this. Don't tell me you were expecting some hot-house bloom?'

'To my shame, I have to confess that must have been the vision in my mind.'

'Well then, you were bound to be disappointed.'

'Oh, I'm not disappointed. Not in the least.' He bent forward to take a closer look at this delicate little flower standing bravely in a crevice in the rock, its miniature white petals nodding gently when the breeze crept into its hiding place. 'But you have to admit, Catrin, there is something a little ridiculous about an entire army of grown men fighting each other over something no bigger than a finger.'

'I've heard diamonds are small, too, and that they cause whole wars.'

'Yes. Yes, of course you're right.' Another cloud enveloping them, leaving their faces shining with tiny water droplets. Philip frowned, suddenly serious. 'Are you sure about this, Catrin? It will take some time, you know. Taking risks is in Judith's blood, and I'm the fool who agreed to help her. You didn't agree to any of this. I don't want to put you in danger. If you say so, I'll swear blind the lilies here were faded. Dead, even. It's not as if Judith has any hope of winning this prize, anyhow. I expect Sullivan is half-way to the train by now.'

Catrin swallowed. 'This means nothing to him,' she reminded herself. 'And tomorrow he will be gone, whatever happens, and I will never see him again.' It suddenly felt as if a vast emptiness had opened up before her. 'I'm quite sure,' she replied, aloud. 'And anyhow, Judith would never forgive you.' He scrutinised her face once more.

'Very well,' he said, at last. 'In that case, you'd better help me set up this equipment. The sooner we finished the portrait of the Snowdon Lily and are on our way back, the better.'

10

'Well?' Judith demanded, as the two re-appeared at the edge of the rock. 'Was it there?'

'A perfect specimen,' called Philip. 'I've exposed three plates. At least one of them should provide us with a good print for the Cambrian Society.'

'Good, good.' Judith let out an audible sigh of relief. 'Well, hurry, then. There's no time to lose.'

Philip and Catrin exchanged smiles at this impatience.

'Just don't smash anything on the way down,' said Catrin, as Philip tied the rope around his waist once more and prepared to lower himself over the edge to begin the long climb to safety.

'That is definitely more than my life is worth,' he returned, wryly. He took her hand. 'Catrin — '

'You must hurry, Philip. If this cloud

gets any thicker it will be impossible to find our way down to the guesthouse tonight.'

For a moment he seemed about to argue with her. But then he nodded. 'Very well. But don't think for a moment this is the end. We have unfinished business, you and I. And I hate to leave anything unfinished.'

Catrin watched, letting the rope play slowly through her hands as he moved down the rock face step by painful step, taking care not to jolt the precious glass negatives in his backpack. She was tired, and growing shivery as the damp of the mist penetrated her dress and through her underclothes, leaving her skin chilled and clammy.

A tight knot of fear was back in her belly, tightening further each time a new cloud swept around her, obliterating Philip completely from her sight for minutes on end, leaving only the taughtness of the rope in her hands to let her know he was still alive.

She wanted to be down from here,

and off the mountain as quickly as possible. And yet there was a part of her that had wished these past few hours would never end. They had worked fast, the two of them, to take the photograph of the lily before the light became too dim for the camera to work.

The process had fascinated her, although at the same time she couldn't help wondering why anyone would wish to take a photograph at all, the cumbersome, time-consuming procedure that it was.

Catrin had come across several painters during her trips to Snowdon, and she couldn't help feeling that they were far less encumbered with their pencils and paper, and small boxes of watercolours. Why on earth, she wondered, would anyone go to all the trouble of photography, when the pictures weren't even going to show any colour? They were real, Philip had tried to explain.

Exactly what you could see with your eyes, not someone's drawing, which could never be real, like that. And once you made one negative, you could make hundreds of prints, all exactly the same.

Which all sounded very strange to Catrin. She felt a tugging on the rope, and realised that Philip had reached the bottom of the cliff. Well, there was nothing for it. With a sigh, she untied the rope from its anchor and secured it firmly round her waist. Then, taking a deep breath, she forced her aching limbs over the ledge of the rock, her feet feeling for the first foothold to start her on her way down.

⋆ ⋆ ⋆

'I can never thank you enough,' said Judith, as Catrin slithered down the last few feet to land beside her. 'We couldn't have done this without you. What can I possibly say?'

'There is no need,' said Catrin, winding the rope around her arm as swiftly as possible. Every part of her seemed to ache unbearably, and her legs were trembling slightly with the effort of making her way down. But she was all too aware that there was no time for any of them to rest. 'You can thank me when we get back to the guest-house.' She gave a quick smile. 'When we are all safe and warm. Come on, we'd better get going.'

Judith frowned at her. 'Surely you need to rest?'

'I'll be fine.' Catrin tied the coiled rope to her backpack, and lifted it on to her aching shoulders. 'We need to get down below this mist before it gets any thicker.'

Thankfully, Judith appeared to understand the urgency. Catrin had no energy left to argue with an imperious young woman used to having her own way. She would need all the energy and concentration left in her for the task ahead.

'Agreed.' Philip was on his feet and settling his heavy pack on his shoulders. 'I don't like the idea of spending the night up here. Or waiting until the mist clears.' Judith had already shrugged herself into the straps of her own backpack, and was retrieving her walking cane from between two rocks.

'Very well. Let's find our way back to the path,' she said.

⋆ ⋆ ⋆

Progress was painfully slow. Catrin picked her way carefully back between the maze of boulders, peering through the mist for familiar marks on the rocks. They were now surrounded completely in a world of white that deadened all sound and left their voices echoing in the air, as if there was nothing real left in the world, just the three of them wandering along through a vast emptiness of white.

Occasionally, the wind stirred, revealing the cliffs rising up above them, and the rocks stretching out below them. Once, the cloud parted completely, revealing the gleam of the green water of the lake and the rise of mountains all around them, bathed in the warm glow of evening sunshine.

'If we can just get below the cloud,' Catrin told herself, establishing her bearings as much as she could in the brief moment of clarity. At least they seemed to be still heading in the right direction.

'We should cut straight down,' said Judith, as if reading her thoughts. 'At least then we will be able to see where we are going.'

'It's too risky,' Catrin replied. 'It's not as straightforward as it looks: there are gullies and crevices in the rocks, as well as cliffs you don't see until you are right on top of them.'

'We're all experienced. All we need is to be careful.'

'It's easy to get to a place where there is no way out, which forces you to retrace your steps back up the mountainside,' said Catrin. 'Besides, if we leave the path it will be difficult for anyone to find us.'

'Find us?'

'Of course. My father knows we're off the main path in the mist. He'll be sending as many men as can be spared to find us the moment he reaches Pen-y-pass.

'Oh.' Judith drew in a breath, as if to offer further reasons for branching off down to the lake.

'Catrin is our guide,' said Philip, quietly. 'She found the lily for us. I suggest we trust her judgement in this, too. You are not leader of this expedition, Judith.'

There was a moment's silence.

'Very well,' said Judith, at last. 'I'm hungry,' she added, beginning to unfasten her pack.

'Have this, then.' Catrin found Philip handing her a small package from his pocket. 'Bara — what did you call it, Catrin?'

'*Bara Brith*. It means 'spotted bread'. Because of the currants.'

'And very tasty it is too. And don't think I shan't be demanding your share, Judith, once we get to a place we can sit down and rest for a bit,' he added.

Judith laughed, all argument forgotten. 'You might have to fight me for it,' she replied. Philip smiled.

Catrin hitched her backpack to a more comfortable position, determination flooding through her once more. However tired she got, she wasn't going to stop or give in until they were out of this mist and within sight of safety.

She turned back, trying to keep in her mind the wind of the little path as it made its way beneath the summit and along to the main route, and began to plod steadily along.

The cloud was growing denser by the minute. There were no more swirls to break its grip apart for even the smallest moment. By now, they could scarcely see a few paces in front of their feet. Rocks loomed out at them, abruptly, appearing dark and ominous in the pallor of the world around them.

Sheep, searching for the meagre grass amongst the stones, stopped to stare at the strange creatures suddenly upon them, before turning to leap recklessly out of sight, tails bobbing as they fled.

The rocks were now clammy with damp, and slippery beneath their feet. They had slowed even further, feeling their way cautiously along, each one of them all-too aware of the dangers of a twisted ankle or a broken bone. Catrin pulled herself carefully past the next boulder, and frowned at the network of rock ahead of her.

'It has to be here,' she muttered. 'This has to be the right way.' She looked back at Judith and Philip, arriving next to her. 'I know I was right this far.' She gave a grimace. 'It all looks the same in the mist.'

'You're tired.' Philip's voice was reassuring. 'We can't be far off the path, I'm certain. We can rest for a few minutes.'

Catrin hesitated. They must get off the mountain. They were all too exhausted and wet through with sweat and mist to be able to keep themselves warm, however short the night. And, besides, she was now so tired, she was afraid if she stopped she would never be able to start again. But, on the other hand, Philip was right, they were all growing too tired to continue. Much more of this and one of them was bound to stumble.

'Very well,' she said. 'But not long enough to get too cold.'

'Agreed,' said Judith.

They each removed their backpacks, sighing at the easing of their shoulder muscles, and propped themselves against the rocks, careful not to lose sight of each other. Tiredly, they each retrieved their small remaining pieces of the day's food, forcing themselves to eat to keep total exhaustion at bay. For a while, they sat there in silence.

'It won't take long once we get to the path,' said Catrin, as cheerfully as she could, praying she had not taken an impossible detour and was leading her companions deeper into the mountain.

Judith sighed, munching on a piece of cheese without enthusiasm.

'I suppose Richard will be roasting himself in front of a fire and toasting his success in champagne,' she said, gloomily. 'It is so unfair. He has more money than he knows what to do with. What could he possibly need with the prize?' Catrin met Philip's eyes. To prevent Judith from having the money, and the freedom it would buy, was the answer that flashed between them. Not that either of them had any desire to voice this in front of Judith.

'You'll find some other way of raising the money,' said Philip.

'How? You just tell me how? I'm not allowed to take paid work. And even if I did, what am I qualified to do? Embroider handkerchiefs and make polite conversation. How could I even feed myself, let alone raise the money for an expedition?

'We could find some other buyer for the picture of the lily. Or maybe guidebooks. Along with the landscapes I've photographed. Guidebooks are all the rage, now, Judith.'

'I'm not taking your money!' Judith frowned. 'You only just earn enough to keep yourself, since you stopped doing all those society portraits.'

'Then I'll begin them again.'

'Don't be ridiculous. You hated them, every one.' She looked out wistfully into the surrounding mist. 'No, I shall just have to do as father wishes. Oh, not Richard. Nothing on earth would induce me to marry Richard.' A hard look came into her eyes. 'No, I shall find someone immensely old and immensely rich, who just won't be able to stand in my way. And I don't care what scandal I cause.'

'You couldn't really marry someone just for their money,' said Catrin, horrified. Judith's face, she saw, was set.

'Why ever not? What other choice do I have? Not unless a miracle should happen, and I don't believe in miracles any more.' She raised her chin, defiantly. 'Anyhow, I bet you'd do the same, Catrin.'

'No,' said Catrin, softly. 'No, that's

something I could never do.'

'Oh, don't tell me you believe in true love and happily ever after,' said Judith, bitterly.

Catrin stared out into the mist in front of her, painfully aware of Philip's eyes boring into her, and the colour rising to her cold cheeks.

'Yes,' she answered, at last. 'Yes, I think I do.'

'Well the more fool you,' snorted Judith.

Catrin gave a wry laugh. 'Most probably,' she replied, dryly. Judith turned to her, suddenly ashamed of her own bad temper.

'No you're not, Catrin. Don't take any notice of me. I was just being horrible. You're not a fool. In fact you're the one of the best people I've ever met, and I hope you really will marry for love and be as happy as can be. Don't you, Philip?'

'Naturally,' he murmured.

'And anyhow, I expect you have lots of really nice young men falling over you, Catrin.' Judith gave a deep sigh. 'Much more than me. Don't you think so, Philip?'

'I — ' he began, awkwardly.

'Listen!' Catrin was on her feet in an instant.

Judith turned. 'What is it?'

'Voices. I'm sure I heard voices.'

'It's Richard. I know it is. Or that Taran fellow.' Judith's voice rose in alarm. 'I knew he wouldn't leave it at that, I just knew he wouldn't.'

'It isn't Richard, Judith. How could it be? No-one could find us in the mist.'

'But then — ' Judith came to an abrupt halt as Catrin began to laugh. 'What is it?'

'It's your miracle,' replied Catrin, already reaching for her backpack. 'Look.' She pointed through the mist. Barely visible, a figure was moving through, followed by a second, then a third, vanishing in a moment. 'The path. We've reached the path. We must be sitting right at the side of it.'

A rattle of stones came from high

above, followed by the murmur of voices far below.

'Close together. Keep close together,' came a man's voice through the cloud.

Catrin gave a sigh of relief, while the tiredness of a few minutes ago seemed to have vanished.

'Come on,' she said. 'Let's get out of this, and see what can be done with those photographs of yours.'

11

'I thought you'd never be getting off the mountain before nightfall, *cariad*.' Will Owen hugged his daughter tightly with his good arm. 'I was that worried, I was, when I saw the old Brenin Llwyd coming down from the summit.'

Catrin smiled. 'Well the Grey King wouldn't hurt me, Dad. He knows I'm a Snowdon girl, born and bred.'

'And I should hope not, too. Now pull your chair closer to the fire, and get yourself properly warm. Mari will be ready with her good hot cawl in a moment. That should banish the mountain air from your innards.'

'Yes, Dad.' Catrin held her blue and stiffened fingers out towards the blissful heat from the logs piled high in readiness for their arrival, wincing as the blood began to painfully flow through them once more.

The last rays of sun had been fading from the lower slopes of Snowdon as the little party emerged from the mist into a gilded world of grasses, with bees hovering busily amongst the purple expanses of heather. The evening air had felt deliciously warm, even in the shadow of the mountain, but, like her companions, Catrin had been too weary and too chilled to the bone from the dampness of her clothing to gain any benefit from the echoes of the day's heat.

By the time they had stumbled down the last section of the path, to be met by an assembled group of guides who, having already brought their tourists down to safety, were all ready to ascend once more into the mist in search of Will Owen's daughter, all three of them could scarcely put one foot in front of the other. Even Philip had been persuaded to relinquish his precious backpack, while Judith had made no bones about leaning heavily on her stick.

Catrin had not been able to rest, despite the reassurances of the guides, until they were back in the guesthouse once more and she had seen with her own eyes Dad beaming happily at her, his ribs heavily bandaged and his arm in a sling.

Her fingers had lost all feeling, and she had been forced to call on Mari to help her out of her sodden dress and petticoats, and fasten the dry clothing waiting for her. Mari was now helping Judith, who had muttered that she could manage very well on her own, thank you, but had not continued with her protests when Mari had tapped timidly on her door as Catrin made her way down to the fire.

* * *

Catrin sighed. She could hear footsteps creaking on the boards in the rooms above. She was far too comfortable to move, while the feeling was creeping back into her fingers and toes once more. But she could hear a door opening, and footsteps on the stairs.

'I'd better go and make sure that the soup isn't burning,' she muttered.

'You'll do no such thing.' Dad pushed her back into the chair as she made to rise. 'John is playing cook until Mari has finished with Miss Meredith. All he has to do is to stir, and watch that the bread isn't burning.' He grinned. 'It will help keep his mind off his guests who haven't made it down yet,' he added.

'*Duw*, he should know by now these fern hunters just never give up, mist or no mist, until the last light of day. They've good guides with them, they'll be down, safe enough.'

He looked up as Philip, closely followed by his sister and Mari, made his way into the room. 'Come in, come in. There are chairs ready for you here, and a hot cup of tea brewing in the pot for you.'

Mari vanished in the direction of the kitchen, to rescue her cawl from Uncle

John's tender mercies. A smell of fresh bread soon began to pervade the air, reminding Catrin of just how empty her stomach was by now. She smiled at Judith, who was also smelling the air, hungrily.

'I could eat a horse,' she announced, loudly, abandoning all pretence of a chair, instead crouching down as close to the flames as she could get.

'Knowing you, Judith, you probably would,' replied Philip, with a smile. 'I don't know how you can spend your life dreaming of days like this one. Snowdon is quite enough for me. I have no wish whatsoever to go clambering about in the snow in your precious Alps.'

'Yes you would, once you got there,' his sister retorted. She sighed. 'And, anyhow, you don't have to find out now. The London train will just be departing. I expect Richard will be opening his first bottle of champagne by now.'

'Not necessarily,' murmured Will, gazing absently into the flames.

Catrin eyed him, sharply. 'How do you mean, 'not necessarily?' '

Dad was grinning. 'Well, as I told you, my dear, the road is rough and perilous through the mountains and all kinds of things can happen.'

'Not that perilous.' Catrin watched him with suspicion. 'Tourists go to and fro every day at this time of year.'

'Ah yes, well, *cariad*, but accidents do happen.'

'Accidents?' Judith looked up from the fire.

'An overturned carriage. A broken wheel. That kind of thing. Don't you agree, John?' he added to his brother, emerging from the kitchen with a very large teapot steaming merrily away.

'Terrible thing a broken wheel,' came the reply, with a slow shaking of the head. 'A few bolts come loose and a rough road, and, well, a man could find himself flung into a ditch on an out-of-the-way place across the moors, with the driver gone off for assistance and nothing to do but to sit it out until morning.'

'And then a wait for help to come. And that before the mending, and the arrival of new horses. You can't expect horses out all night in the cold to be pulling a carriage in this kind of country.'

'Dad!' Catrin shook her head, slowly.

'But you can't be sure something like that could have happened to Mr Sullivan,' said Philip, eyeing the two men closely. 'No-one could have got a message back so quickly.'

John laid the teapot down on the table where cups and saucers were already waiting.

'*Duw* no, of course not. No way of knowing.' He gave a broad wink. 'Not unless you happened to be sending a telegraph message to an inn along the route, one particularly favoured by carriage drivers, and just happened to get a message back.'

He rubbed his hands on his jacket and prepared to return to the kitchen.

'Useful things, these new telegraph messages,' he added, thoughtfully.

'But won't they be suspicious?' demanded Philip.

'*Duw*, I very much doubt it, young man. Rough road, wild countryside. Savage natives who don't speak English. From what I saw of your Mr Sullivan, I suspect it's just the sort of thing he might be expecting. And why should he worry overmuch? He has the photograph and the lily has been destroyed. Just a little delay, that's all.'

Judith and Philip exchanged glances. Judith's eyes were glowing once more. She stood up.

'Then we have to go. Leave at once,' she said. 'We shall have to find a carriage for hire — ' she was striding across the room already, making for the staircase. 'Come on, Philip. We have to pack. We've no time to lose.'

'Now there's no hurry, Miss Meredith,' said Dad, disapproval appearing in his face. 'And you can't be setting out half frozen and without a good hot meal inside you.'

'We can eat all we wish once we get to London,' she retorted, impatiently. Philip gave a resigned sigh, and rose slowly to his feet.

'You can eat while the carriage is being prepared,' said Dad. They both turned to look at him. 'So long as you set off within the hour you'll be sure to get through in time for the next train. I'm quite certain Mr Sullivan won't find himself so fortunate until at least midday tomorrow.'

Philip chuckled. 'I'm not sure I'd like to get on the wrong side of you, Mr Owen,' he said.

'*Duw*, no. You need have no fear of that,' replied Dad, with a smile. 'Ah, now here's Mari with the soup. It'll do us all good to have a good hot meal inside us. Make you able to face anything, it will.'

Catrin sighed as she stepped outside into the night. The wind had died down, leaving clouds stranded in the sky, glowing silver in the faint light of the quarter moon. Mist still hung around the higher reaches of Snowdon, with long thin silvers resting in dips in the rock, and down in the valley below, towards Beddgelert.

Silence hung in the air, despite the bustle behind her, as trunks were being lifted onto the back of the carriage and strapped firmly in place, filling her with a strange sense of restlessness.

'Beautiful, isn't it?' She turned as Philip, almost completely enveloped in a large overcoat, paused behind her.

'Very,' she replied.

'I'm sorry we have to leave so quickly.'

'Of curse you have to, if you are to have a chance of winning the prize.'

'Judith asked me to make sure and thank you on behalf of both of us. You made us achieve the impossible, Catrin.'

'You were the one who took the pictures,' she replied. 'But I enjoyed it. Every moment of it. Well, at least almost every moment of it. And I hope you get the photograph to the Royal Cambrian Society first.'

'I'm sure you'll hear about it if we do.' There was a smile in his voice.

'I'm sure I will.' There was a moment's silence between them. Catrin found her hand being felt for, and then lightly clasped in the enveloping darkness.

'Catrin, what I said up there. I meant it, every last word of it.'

'I know.' A terrible emptiness was opening up inside her. Somehow, until this moment, it had not seemed real that he was going. London was a different world, and one so far away Catrin could scarcely imagine it.

She had to face facts, he might think he had feelings for her now, with all that they had shared, and the fear and the danger they had been through together these past few hours. But once back in his own world, what reason would he have to remember her at all?

Apart from a vague sentimental memory of a Welsh girl he might have fancied himself attracted to for a brief moment of time. *But I will never forget you*, her heart cried out inside her. 'The carriage must be ready,' she said, aloud, to cover the trembling in her limbs, and to fight back a sudden threat of tears.

'I wish — '

She placed her hand swiftly over his mouth. 'Don't wish,' she said, softly. 'You have no need to wish for anything at all.' She found her hand being gently removed and taken to his lips.

'Philip!' It was Judith, framed in the light of the doorway, peering out impatiently into the darkness. 'We have to go now, Philip. There is no time to lose.'

'Good luck,' said Catrin, quietly. Her hand was still held prisoner. 'And I will never forget this. Any of this.'

'Neither will I,' he replied. For the briefest of moments, his lips found hers, and then he was gone.

Within minutes the carriage door had shut upon its occupants, and the little vehicle was making its way down slowly, the way it had come, twisting and winding down the steep little track towards Beddgelert, far below, and to the train ready to take them back to London.

12

Catrin plodded slowly up the track from Llanberis towards Pen-y-Pass. All around her, the russet shades of autumn had settled over the hillsides, turning the mountains to gold, punctuated by the deep red of rowan berries and the fiery shades of oak and beech.

She was glad the season for visitors was almost over, and that this would be her last few days at Uncle John's guesthouse before the snow and ice of the winter months made it almost inaccessible. She was tired, she found, in a way she had never felt before. Tired of this journey. Tired of the smell of cooking, and the endless cleaning and chopping of vegetables.

She would watch the mountaineers heading for the summit with barely disguised envy, and pause, unable to move when she passed them on their return, drinking in the faint scents of the mountain air that still clung to them as they laughed around the fire, swapping stories of their impossible feats of the day.

No, she decided, for once she would be glad to retreat back down to the cottage in Llanberis for the winter, and bury herself in the endless task of keeping the house in order, and Dad and Nain fed and warm.

'Maybe I'll find something closer to Llanberis, next summer,' she thought to herself. 'There must be hotels and guesthouses nearby that are in need of a cook. Or maybe I should try along the coast. There are plenty of hotels in Conwy.'

Of course, that would mean she would have to live away from home for weeks on end, Conwy being so far away. But it might be just what she needed, a touch of something new. And at least there, the visitors' talk would all be of the castle, and not of the mountains.

'Catrin . . . '

She paused at the familiar figure waiting for her at the side of the track as she passed the entrance to Aunt Margaret's farm.

'Hello Guto,' she replied, with a smile. Guto had grown bolder these last few weeks, without the mocking gaze of his father to throw him off his stride. This time he was practically blocking her way forward, his hands twirling his discarded hat between them, nervously.

'Catrin . . . '

'Yes, Guto?'

'I was wondering . . . ' Guto blushed to the roots of his hair, and a look of desperation came into his face.

Catrin smiled at him in what she hoped was an encouraging manner, without being too encouraging and giving him entirely the wrong idea.

'It's my sister. She's getting married this time next week.' He came to a flustered halt, as if overcome by his own boldness.

'Yes, I know. I'm one of her bridesmaids,' said Catrin, carefully repressing a broader smile.

'Oh. Yes. Of course. Of course you are.' He stepped back, as if to leave it at that. Catrin took a few steps forward.

'Good day, Guto,' she said.

'Catrin — '

She turned. Guto took the deepest breath he could manage. 'Catrin, I thought, perhaps, if you wish to, you might like to dance with me.' His good-natured face wrinkled up in anxiety. 'Only if you want to, that is.'

'I thought you were dancing with Sioned Pierce for every dance?' said Catrin, gently. She didn't like to add that Mari's pretty cousin was known as a determined young woman, who had set her sights on taking Guto firmly in hand for years.

Besides, it was well known that you didn't cross swords with a Pierce — it least not where eligible young men with a very presentable farm to inherit from an elderly aunt were concerned.

'Oh, yes.' Depression settled on Guto's brow. For which, thought Catrin to herself, there was really no need. Sioned might prove ruthless where catching a future husband was concerned, but she was good-humoured and lively on all other occasions, and clearly possessed of enough determination to make both herself and Guto amongst the richest farmers in the valley one day. Catrin found his eyes pleading with her. 'But at least one dance, Catrin. I don't mind if it's just the one . . . '

Catrin couldn't resist. 'Of course, Guto. I'd be delighted.'

Guto heaved a deep sigh. 'I'm glad. I'm really so glad. It will mean so much to me, Catrin.'

'I must go, Guto. I'll be late.'

'Oh, yes. Yes, of course. Goodbye, Catrin.'

'Goodbye,' called Catrin, escaping quickly, before her smile could get out of her control. Poor Guto! She was touched by his undisguised devotion, but she knew it would only be one dance.

Sioned Pierce apart, Catrin felt deep in her heart that she could never be happy with Guto, working the farm on Snowdon's slopes with a crowd of children at her heels. And she had a suspicion that, should Guto ever get to know her better, she would hurt and perplex him with her restlessness and her wistful gaze up towards Snowdon's summit and her dreams.

Catrin pulled herself together, and, putting her thoughts firmly from her mind, she made her way quickly to the guesthouse.

'Not a bedroom free?' Catrin gazed at Mari in astonishment. 'But it's never this busy, this late in the year.'

'I told you we'd be full, with all that fuss over the photograph of the Snowdon Lily,' said Mari, with a chuckle. 'We've had botanists fighting to get up Snowdon, for all your dad keeps telling them they won't hardly find a trace, this time of year. But they all want to gaze up at the place where the picture was taken, all the same.'

'Really?' Catrin bit her lip. 'But he can't!' Mari knew all about Richard Sullivan and his destruction of the lily, surely she must realise . . .

Mari winked. '*Duw*, no. He isn't taking them right up to the place. Told them it's too dangerous this time of year, and will harm the plants. Don't worry, Catrin, they've replaced what they can, and taken a few more from — well, other places. Come next summer no one will be able to spot the difference. And a good things too. Your uncle will be opening on Christmas Day, at this rate.'

'Good.' Catrin was silent for a moment. 'So who is booked in, then?' she asked, keeping her voice casual, as she always did when she asked such a question. She tried to avoid Mari's sharp look.

'Last week's fern-collectors are still here. There's party from Chester booked in till Sunday, and three gentlemen on a walking tour.' Mari nodded at the bags piled up near the front door. 'The carriage will be calling for them in a bit, with the new arrivals to take their place, so we'll need to work sharpish to get their rooms ready.'

'Oh?' Catrin discovered her heart was thumping uncomfortably in her chest. She should know better by now than to run to the window each time the carriage arrived, and to look carefully down the list of names in Uncle John's book in the office.

Judith Meredith was probably stomping her way determinedly over some glacier, heading for a summit that could dwarf Snowdon with ease. And as for her brother — why, he had most likely forgotten her all together.

'Honeymoon couple,' said Mari, with undisguised disapproval. 'With chaperone.' She shook her head. 'I never will understand these rich people, I'll be honest with you, *cariad*. If me and my Gareth had the money, we'd be going somewhere nice and hot, with a few old temples to look around, not halfway up Snowdon. And not with a chaperone. Can you imagine it? Over my dead body.'

She looked up as the distant rattle of wheels over stone drifted towards them. 'That must be them now. They're nearly an hour late, I was beginning to despair of them, to tell the truth.' She grinned. 'Though maybe this business of wheels falling off in inconvenient places might be catching.'

Catrin laughed. 'I sincerely hope not. That will be no good at all for Uncle John's business,' she said, before ducking hastily into the kitchen out of the way, as the rush of footsteps on the stairs told her that the walking tour gentlemen had also spotted the approaching carriage, and were determined to have no delay that might cause them to miss their train.

As they gathered their belongings together, she grasped the basket of clean linen waiting for her, and slipped quickly up to make the rooms as clean and presentable as she could in the short time left to her.

When Catrin re-emerged, the carriage had halted next to the front door, and was disgorging its passengers, along with what looked like a small mountain of trunks, while the trunks of the departing gentlemen were being secure in their place.

Smoothing down her apron, she moved forward to greet the bride, who was dressed from head to toe in pink silk, and appeared very young and half terrified out of her wits by the lurching past cliff-edges of the past hour or so.

'*Duw* no, girl. You haven't stopped since you've arrived. You go into the kitchen and make yourself a *panad*. I'll deal with this lot.' Mari shook her head as a second figure emerged from the carriage. 'And a proper gorgon that one looks, and no mistake. That poor child, I don't expect she had any say in this at all, and she looks as if she could do with a good dose of sun, so she does, poor thing.'

Without giving Catrin a chance to reply, Mari was off towards the new arrivals, as if bent on rescuing the unfortunate young bride single-handedly. Catrin smiled to herself as the vision in pink was firmly removed from her husband and chaperone, and led up towards the guesthouse, as the departing guests pulled the door of the carriage too, and the horses were chivvied up into life once more.

'And will she faint away, do you suppose?' Catrin started. She must be dreaming. Or the mountain was playing tricks on her — she swung round.

'Philip!' he was standing behind her, the faintly amused smile she remembered all too well on his face.

'What do you think?' He took a step closer. 'Personally speaking, I think that young lady might be made of sterner stuff than first appears. They often are, you know. My bet is, she'll be rushing up Snowdon in a day or so leaving those two far behind.'

'Philip, what on earth are you doing here?'

'Watching my friends depart.'

'Your friends?'

'Yes. I do have them you know, Catrin. And I am a free agent, so quite entitled to embark on a walking tour with two of them.'

'But the coach — ' She looked at him in bewilderment.

'Didn't Mari tell you? I'm booked in for a full week more. I'm surprised you didn't know, Catrin. Mari did mention you quiz her very carefully each time you arrive.'

'I do not! And anyhow, I have to know who our guests are.' She frowned at him. 'And now you're laughing at me.'

'I would never laugh at you, Catrin. I just can't quite believe you really are here. I was so afraid your father would send a message down to you to prevent you coming today. He's been watching me with great suspicion all week.' Catrin caught the look in his eyes and her legs began to shake.

'I must go,' she said, quickly. 'It's Mari's time to go home.'

'Mari loves you, and wants your happiness,' he replied. 'She and I have come to a little, um, arrangement concerning this evening. Although she will still need to get home before it is dark,' he added, regretfully.

Catrin discovered joyful laughter beginning to bubble up inside her. 'You mean, you have resorted to bribery, Mr Meredith?'

'I knew you'd understand.' His smile had broadened, while the intensity of his eyes had deepened. Catrin felt her whole body tremble. 'It's why my sister likes you so much. And why she went me on a mission to request that you join her next expedition. After all, without you, she never would have won the Royal Cambrian Botanical Society prize and been able to make the climb at all.'

Catrin stood there, dazed, the breath knocked out of her. Judith's expedition?

She was being offered a chance to join her? To climb a mountain so high the snow never melted, even in the hottest days of summer? The prospect was beyond her wildest dreams. She should have been jumping for joy, but instead, she felt her heart grow heavy inside her.

'I'm flattered. I really am. I'd love to, of course . . . '

'But?'

'How can I, Mr Meredith? My life is here. Besides, my father would never allow it.'

'And that is the message you want me to take back with me?'

'Yes. No!' She felt tears begin to fill her eyes. She turned away, too proud to let him see them fall. 'No. You know I can't go, Philip. Why are you tormenting me like this?'

'Catrin!' He was next to her, his voice very gentle. 'Catrin, I'm not tormenting you. I would never do anything to hurt you. Not intentionally. Why do you think I jumped at Judith's mission for me?' He was now so close his breath was warm on her face. ‘Catrin, I came to see you. From the moment I left, I haven’t been able to get you out of my mind. You changed my life, you know, in more ways than one.

‘If it hadn’t been for you, I’d still be taking portraits of spoilt dogs and children and pompous old men, instead of being commissioned to photograph flowers and landscapes all over the world.’ He smiled. ‘Judith might think she’s the one asking you to join her, but I am the one who is hanging on your every word.’

‘You?’

‘Of course. Didn’t you read in the papers that Judith will be on a commission from the Royal Cambrian Botanical Society? She will be able to continue her expeditions as long as she wishes, so long as she takes a few botanists along with her. I’ve been commissioned to photograph their findings.

‘I haven’t agreed yet, I needed to speak to you first. Catrin, if your heart is really set against going with my sister — '

'I might be persuaded,' she replied, quietly, lifting up her face to meet his.

'Catrin, I'm a struggling photographer, and I will be for years to come. I can't promise you jewels or fine houses, or an introduction into Society — '

'Philip, you don't honestly think that matters to me, do you?'

'I thought not. I hoped not. In fact, all I hoped for . . . ' His voice was muffled in her hair.

'Yes?' she murmured.

'All I hoped for was that you could find it in your heart to love me, and to agree to be my wife.' He took her face between his hands, his dark eyes gazing into her. 'Say 'yes' Catrin. If I can have any hope at all for your love, put me out of my misery and say that one word. That's all I ask.'

Catrin smiled, happiness flooding through her, relaxing her body against his.

'Oh, I think I can do rather better

than that,' she replied, softly, slipping her arms around his neck, and drawing him towards her, until his lips met hers in a loving kiss.

THE END

Other titles in the Linford Romance Library:

DARK MOON

Catriona McCuaig

When her aunt dies, Jemima is offered a home with her stern uncle, but vows to make her own way in the world by working at a coaching inn. She falls for the handsome and fascinating Giles Morton, but he has a menacing secret that could endanger them both. When Jemima is forced to choose between her own safety and saving the man she loves, she doesn't hesitate for a moment — but will they both come out of it alive?